Cowboys in Her Heart

Cowboys Online : Moose Ranch, Volume 4

Jan Springer

Published by Jan Springer, 2020.

Cowboys in Her Heart ~ Moose Ranch
Cowboys Online 4
Published by Spunky Girl Publishing
Copyright 2017 by Jan Springer
Discover other titles by Jan Springer at http://www.janspringer.com
Cover Art by Talina Perkins, Bookin It Designs

Also by Jan Springer

Club Rendezvous
Shy Girl

Cowboys Online
Her Forever Cowboys

Cowboys Online Italiano
Tre Cowboy per Natale

Cowboys Online : Moose Ranch
Cowboys for Christmas
Cowboys In Her Pocket
Loving Her Cowboys
Cowboys in Her Heart
Always Her Cowboys
Claiming Her Cowboys

Intimate Secrets

Intimate Lover

Intimate Kisses

Intimate Stranger

Kidnap Fantasies

Jade's Fantasy

Zero To Sexy

Christmas Lovers

Pleasure Bound

A Hero's Welcome

A Hero Escapes

A Hero Betrayed

A Hero's Kiss

A Hero Wanted

Captive Heroes

Pleasure Bound Boxed Set

Pleasure Bound : COMPLETE SERIES SciFi Erotic Romance Boxed Set

Tentacles Shifter Erotic Romance

Taken by Him

The Desperadoes

The Pleasure Girl

In Her Bed

Awakening Eve

The Key Club

A Merry Menage Christmas

Sophie's Menage

Jewel's Menage

Jaxie's Menage

The Outlaw Lovers

Jude Outlaw

The Claiming

Colter's Revenge

Tyler's Woman

Resistance

The Outlaw Lovers

Alpha Outlaws Boxed Set

Vampira

Sweet Heat

Dark Heat

Wet Heat

Crimson Heat

Standalone

A Touch of Menage Boxed Set

Shades of Menage Boxed Set

Naughty Girl Desires Boxed Set

Nice Girl Naughty

Sinderella Sexy

The Biker and The Bride

The Fire Within

Bared to Him

Pleasure Bound : A Futuristic Adult Romance Boxed Set

Merry Menage Kisses Boxed Set

Inner Girl Rising

Stripped Naked

Risqué Girl Delights Boxed Set

A Holiday Menage

Ménage À Trois

A Hitman for Hannah

Billionaire Boyfriend

Edible Delights

Vampira

Toygasm

The Dark Side

Watch for more at www.janspringer.com.

Licence Notes
This ebook is permitted for your personal use only.

Author Note
This is a work of fiction. Characters, places, settings and events presented in this book are purely of the author's imagination and bear no resemblance to any actual person, living or dead or to any actual events, places and/or settings.

Chapter One

EARLY JUNE

Moose Ranch, Northern Ontario, Canada

"Are these the plans for the cabin you'll be building this summer?" JJ asked as she gazed over Brady's shoulder. He sat at the dining room table with a large hand-sketched blueprint spread out across the table. A table that she needed to get set up for dinner.

"Yep, that's it. We figured it was best to keep the cabin small and simple. We're placing it close to the lake so you can pick us up with the plane when the cattle drives are over."

The interior layout of the cabin looked pretty good, but she wanted her men to have the best.

"Hmm," JJ muttered as she studied the sketch.

Brady twisted in his chair and frowned as he looked up at her.

"What do you mean, hmm? You don't like it?" he asked with a frown. His blue eyes twinkled with curiosity.

"Oh, I like it. But you'll be spending quite some time there during other trips to check on the cattle and then there is haying in the area and come autumn a one week stretch there every year rounding up the cattle. I think this cabin should be a bit more...homey."

Brady chuckled. The sweet sound sent sparkles of happiness into her. His eyebrows furrowed as he studied her.

"Homey? What exactly does that mean?"

"Cozier. You need fireplaces so we can sit and watch the flames. You should have a fireplace in the living room and one in the bedroom."

He shook his head.

"Fireplaces aren't really practical. Woodstoves give off more heat."

"Fireplace inserts will make them practical. Remember we can fly everything in now. Oh, and how about a nice little outdoor barbecue area in back so I can cook up some steaks. I mean you did say I was coming along on the next cattle drive, right?"

"You did say that she could come along, Brady" Dan chuckled as he walked into the kitchen.

"And you also said she could have everything her little heart desires when it came to decorating all the buildings on the property," Rafe said as he joined them.

Emotions and arousal pummelled her as both Rafe and Dan swooped in close. Dan hugged her first. His strong arms made her feel safe and protected and she never wanted him to let her go.

"I missed you like crazy, baby," Dan whispered into her ear.

When he let her go, Rafe quickly embraced her and kissed her sweetly on her mouth. Her lips tingled and her thoughts were scattering by the time he was finished.

"Man, I've been needing that since I've been gone, sweetheart," Rafe muttered as he held her tight. His dark brown eyes promised there would be more of those kisses coming tonight.

She inhaled deeply. They always smelled so wonderful when they came in from working outdoors. Sweat, fresh air and pine never smelled so good.

"I've missed you two, too," she admitted. "I am glad my guys are all back together where I can keep my eyes on you."

The men chuckled.

Rafe and Dan had been gone for a couple of days checking the herds in the north quarter of the property. Wolves had been a problem all spring, taking down several cows up that way. She was always worried when the guys went out on their trips.

Her uneasiness about their safety while working the wilderness ranch had only increased after that close call with Rafe last year. He'd been seriously injured late last autumn when he'd sliced open his leg with an ax after being interrupted by wolves while he'd been chopping firewood at one of the shelters. With the wolves watching him, he had managed to crawl into a nearby cabin and lain helpless on the floor, needing serious medical attention. When he hadn't called in at an appointed time, they'd gone out looking for him.

But now with all three of her men back home and healthy, she could relax. And they would take turns with her again, whenever she wanted and whenever they wanted her.

JJ swallowed as sensual heat whipped through her. Oh yes, she couldn't wait until tonight. It would be a wonderful welcome home at bedtime. She hurried back into the kitchen so the men wouldn't notice how red her cheeks must be at anticipating what would happen this evening.

"Did you find the nuisance pack of wolves?" Brady asked.

"Yep," Rafe replied. He tossed his knapsack onto the table.

"We caught them in action. They were just about to pounce on the herd when we came along. Boy, did we give them a huge surprise. We popped off a few rounds to scare them. Never seen wolves run so fast," Dan said as he also placed his gear onto the table.

JJ frowned as she retrieved plates from the cupboard. She didn't like the idea of the men alarming the wildlife, but she understood the necessity of frightening them off. She also knew the wolves would be back to hunt down the cattle. Not good for business when wolves, or bears for that matter, began to dine on their herd.

"Get all that stuff off the table or you'll be eating off your knapsacks and those cabin plans," she complained as she brought out the plates and set them beside the cups on the kitchen counter.

There was a shuffle of noise and JJ smiled. She peeked over her shoulder and watched as the three men headed into the living room.

The table had been effectively cleared. Now she could get to the business at hand. She was about to grab the utensils from the drawer, when an odd queasiness whispered through her.

"Oh," she whispered, and her hand flew to her suddenly upset tummy.

"JJ?" Dan must have heard her because he was suddenly jumping up from the living room sofa and hurried toward her.

She waved him away.

"It's nothing." She injected a cheeriness into her voice. It was a cheeriness she didn't feel. Not in the least bit.

"You look awful pale, JJ," Dan growled.

She shook her head, but the queasiness only got worse

Oh no.

"Are you having an anxiety attack?" Rafe asked as he and Brady crowded in around her. They were staring at her with such concern she felt horribly guilty for upsetting them.

"No, no. I just got airsick while I was up in the plane this morning." she lied. Why did she just lie?

Oh dear, she couldn't answer any questions. She really *was* going to be sick.

"Set the table and I'll be back in just a minute," she urged.

A weird bitter taste flooded her mouth. Thankfully the guys didn't follow her as she raced to the bathroom. She thought she would vomit, but just as suddenly as it came, her queasiness disappeared.

"Huh, that was weird," she muttered at her reflection in the mirror.

Perspiration glistened like sparkling jewels on her forehead and more beads popped out above her upper lip. She looked pretty pale too. Her legs were shaky and she felt weak. The possibility that she might be pregnant flashed briefly across her radar, but she dismissed it quickly.

Brady had been trying to get her pregnant for several months now, but she continued to get her periods. She just couldn't be pregnant.

So what was her problem with the nausea? This wasn't the first time she'd felt sick. It had happened a few times over the last month or so and then a bit more often over the last few days, but this episode had been the worst yet. A jolt of anxiety zipped through her. Was she maybe seriously ill?

JJ shook her head and immediately went into her avoid-a-panic-attack mode.

She slowed her breathing, inhaling leisurely and deeply. In her mind, she imagined herself at her favorite place where she always felt safe and serene. At the dock down by the lake.

When the guys were away and she needed a quick break from work, she loved to sit on one of the Adirondack chairs. The mild lake breeze would blow against her skin, and she would listen to the waves as they gently lapped against the pontoons of her float plane that she had moored nearby.

The air would be quiet, broken occasionally by the knock knock knock of a woodpecker cracking its beak against a giant pine tree. Or a chipmunk or red squirrel would chatter nearby.

JJ felt herself calming down. She'd learned the breathing and imaginary techniques from a CD, her pilot friend, Kelly had sent to her just this past Christmas.

The CD had helped immensely with her anxiety issues. Just as recalling the techniques she'd committed to memory helped her now.

JJ blew out a breath, turned on the cold water and splashed her face until it was nice and chilled.

"There, now you look better," she said as she smiled at her rosy cheeks.

She sucked in another breath and then blew it out slowly.

It's probably just a bug trying to get me. I'm strong. I can fight it off.

JJ jumped when a knock erupted at the door.

"JJ?" Brady's deep voice called from the other side.

"Come in," she answered.

The door swung open and she swallowed at the dark look on Brady's face. Oh, oh, he wasn't happy about something. Mentally she quickly assessed what she might have done wrong, but came up with nothing.

"Why did you just lie? You told them you took the plane out. I was in the barn all day and I didn't hear the plane."

Oh shoot. Think fast, JJ.

"Sorry, I didn't want you guys to worry. I—"

"You *are* having an anxiety attack, aren't you?" Brady asked, cutting her off and giving her the perfect excuse.

"Actually, yes." Another lie. Oh dear, she was lying way too much.

"Can I help?" he asked as he stepped closer. His brow was furrowed as he studied her.

"I'm better now. I just used some imagery and it helped." At least that part was true.

He smiled and the sweet way his lips curled upwards and the sparkles of love in his blue eyes made her heart beat faster. Gosh, he looked so cute she could just eat him up.

"Don't tell the guys, ok?" she whispered.

"Hmm, I'll have to think of a way to blackmail you in order for you to ensure I keep that secret," he whispered back.

He wanted to kiss her. She could read the twinkles in his eyes. But just as he lowered his head, she side stepped him. If he kissed her, then no one would be getting any supper.

His laughter chased her out the door.

It was Rafe's night with her tonight and she couldn't wait to be with him, JJ thought as she stepped into the steaming shower. They'd agreed to meet in her room tonight. She knew what that meant. Rafe wanted to tie her down and make love to her.

She creamed at that idea and a breathless excitement rushed through her. Still she had trouble believing how, after being incarcerated for ten years and told what to do everyday by the prison guards, that she was now free to do what *she* wanted. And she wanted to live with her three sexy cowboys.

It was sinful. Shocking. And nice having her men paying so much attention to her.

What had she done so *right* in her life to get so lucky? She thought as she hummed happily and soaped her curves, paying extra special attention to her very tender nipples. They were so ultra-sensitive lately. It was almost hurtful when the guys touched her there. But it was a sharp erotic addition to their tender lovemaking.

She'd noticed the guys were a bit overly gentle with her since she'd asked Brady to be the father of her first child. She didn't mind the gentleness. Much.

A tinge of sadness whispered over her at the thought she still wasn't pregnant. Last fall, when she had abruptly decided she wanted a baby with Brady, her decision had felt so right.

She wanted this ranch house filled with her children. With their children. Lots of babies. She wanted a *real* family with the men.

She frowned and stopped humming as she soaped between her thighs. What if she never could have a baby? Maybe all the stress of being in prison for so many years and all the anxiety and panic attacks she had experienced had screwed with her body?

Maybe she was infertile? A rush of panic snapped through her.

Oh no you don't! Reign in that over-active imagination, woman! Her inner voice chastised.

JJ shook her head and stepped beneath the steaming shower spray to allow the water to drown away her insecurities.

If there was one thing she was guilty of, it was her imagination being vivid. She laughed to herself and then shampooed her hair.

"You are just freaking yourself out about everything lately, aren't you?" she mumbled as she quickly washed out the shampoo. She should be the happiest woman alive having three sweet men at her beck and call and—.

She tensed as a shadow moved on the other side of the steamed shower glass door. And then another shadow appeared.

Oh.

She turned to explore who was out there when the shower door suddenly slid open. Rafe stood there. He wore a crooked grin and a very nice erection. Awareness zipped through her as he stepped inside the stall. He was followed by Dan, who was also naked.

Mercy. Their cocks looked thick and hard. Intense excitement flooded her, and JJ licked her lips with anticipation as she saw the rope in Dan's hand. Okay, so much for Rafe tying her to her bed. They were going to tie her in here.

"You were taking too long, sweetheart. I thought I'd bring the party to you, with a little bit of help from the guys and some foreplay," Rafe said as he slipped one end of the rope through a sturdy stainless-steel eyelet located on the ceiling. The guys had installed several eyelets along various areas of the shower stall and JJ had enjoyed many naughty trysts being tied in here with the guys making love to her.

Her breath caught as she spied the leather cuffs at the other end of the rope. She held still as Dan slipped the restraints around her wrists. Then he pulled on the rope which in turn raised her arms upward until her armpits stretched with a sensual burn. The warm water splashed against her upper back, nicely loosening any tense muscles this new position caused.

He tied off the rope to a grab bar.

She enjoyed when they restrained her. Feeling helpless, yet knowing she was very safe with them, shot exquisite desire through her.

Her pussy grew hot and heavy as Dan and Rafe studied her breasts and stroked their engorged cocks.

She tensed as Rafe grabbed the portable showerhead from its perch overhead. He angled the spray over his head soaking his brown hair. Then he squirt a dose of shampoo into his hand. As he kept his brown gaze fixed to hers, he handed the shower head to Dan and then Rafe shampooed his hair.

She blew out harsh pants as she watched the muscles in Rafe's chest and arms bulge with his every movement. Dan joined Rafe, shampooing his own hair while JJ was forced to watch them. There were two gorgeously naked men mere inches from her and she could do nothing!

Oh, come on! They were going to torture her by making her wait until *they* decided it was time to make love to her? The buggers!

Rafe retrieved the showerhead from Dan, and quickly angled the spray over Dan's head rinsing his hair. White bubbly suds dribbled over his nipples and she followed the sudsy trail as it arrowed over Dan's taut belly and into his nest of pubic hair.

JJ's breath caught as Rafe handed Dan a bar of soap and then moved the water jet lower, over Dan's tummy and then sprayed his scrotum. Dan swore softly at the impact and he quickly soaped his sac and then rubbed soap onto the jerking length of his shaft.

Rafe followed up by squirting away the suds. Once again Dan cursed as the water zapped his cock. JJ giggled as Dan, a bit pissed off, tore away the showerhead from Rafe and turned the jet on him. Rafe laughed and quickly soaped his chest and then his ridge-board muscled abdomen. JJ licked her lips as Rafe's penis straightened and engorged even more than before beneath his attentive fingers.

"My own personal tv porn stars," JJ giggled.

"Only, this is real life," Dan growled. He aimed the pulsing water over Rafe's slightly hairy chest and then took his revenge by spurting his cock and scrotum.

"Man! That hurts!" Rafe complained.

Dan laughed and shot water against Rafe's left nipple. He was greeted with another curse.

"Getting crowded in here," Brady's deep voice echoed above the splashes of water as he entered the bathing area. He wore nothing but heavy-lidded blue eyes and a very promising erection.

JJ's pussy clenched at seeing Brady.

"The more the merrier," JJ replied in a husky voice.

She yelped as the spray was suddenly aimed at her tender left nipple.

"It appears we won't be having any water shortages around here," Dan teased as JJ convulsed against the impact.

Rafe laughed and JJ jerked when Brady cupped her right breast, lowered his head, and sucked her nipple into his hot mouth.

Just as quickly, Rafe stepped to her other side. He laved a hot palm under her breast, moved his head closer and slid her right nipple between his warm lips.

She moaned and closed her eyes at the scorching impact of a mouth attached to each nipple.

"Looks like I am missing some action," Dan complained from behind the guys.

JJ tried to respond by telling him to find any spot on her body to suckle, but she couldn't speak. They were sensually massaging her breasts and teasing her very sensitive nipples to the point where she was gasping.

She didn't know how Dan managed to get between Brady and Rafe, but suddenly there were a couple of hands sliding between her thighs. She opened her legs and yelped as a gentle spray of water snapped against her clit. Fiery sensations whipped through her making her quiver and convulse against her restraints.

Dan was using the shower head on her!

The muscles in her abdomen tightened and her pussy clenched at the scorching impact. Then Dan spread her labia and she writhed as the pulsing stream of water entered her vagina. He angled the spray of water to her clit again, tenderly massaging and expertly teasing her sensitive bundle of nerves until her pussy was on fire and she danced against the restraints.

Her heart raced and she bucked as Dan's heated mouth replaced the spray of water. Having three mouths making love to her intimate parts made her blood sing. She was at their mercy as their tongues licked and lapped and their stroking fingers massaged and rubbed until pleasure burned her alive.

Her breaths increased and soon she was keening, needy and begging for that hot and heavy penetration that would bring her release from this sizzling agony.

Suddenly the two men at her breasts let go of her. Her nipples ached and throbbed, and her vagina was hot and sticky from her arousal. She barely noticed that Dan was untying her and then Rafe was leading her out of the stall. She could barely stand on her trembling legs, as Rafe held her arms so the men could towel dry her. Then she heard Dan's and Brady's quiet goodnights as they disappeared from the bathroom.

"Now I have you all to myself," Rafe whispered as he lifted JJ into his arms and carried her into her bedroom.

She whimpered softly in answer. She burned for Rafe. Yearned for him to take her and extinguish the flames that they had created with their hot, probing tongues and heated mouths. Her nipples ached from Rafe and Brady's suckling and her pussy felt puffy and heavy with need.

The soft mattress met her back as Rafe lay her upon her cool sheets. When he settled in beside her, she rolled onto her side and reached out to him. Her fingers dug into his shoulders and she urged him closer. He turned onto his side, facing her. He reached behind her and brought the sheets and blankets over them.

"Hey baby, just wanted to tell you how much I love you," he said softly His brown eyes sparkled with such love it squeezed her heart.

"I love you too, Rafe. So much," she replied.

Happiness and giddiness shifted through her as she watched him sheath his cock with a condom. Then he reached back and shut off the bedside lamp. When he turned to her, she lifted her leg and brought it over his hip. He moved against her and quickly pressed his rigid flesh into her.

She sucked in a breath at the pressure of his engorged shaft sliding into her. He kissed her lips, sweetly and then harshly, and JJ moaned at the tingles and dug her fingers into his taut back drawing him closer. As he slid in deeper, her vaginal muscles protested and then welcomed his thick intrusion.

He groaned as her inner muscles clenched. He quickly rolled both of them until he was on top of her.

He kept kissing her as he withdrew. He moved his chest off hers and erotically rubbed his cock over her clit. As he thrust into her again, he brushed his hairy chest against her already sensitive nipples, creating a sweet shocking pleasure.

He left her and then plunged into her faster and deeper, his thick shaft sparking shudders and pleasure all along the length of her vagina.

They furiously gyrated against each other, each moving closer to their own orgasm. Rafe bucked and pistoned and JJ tensed as arousal built with lightning speed, snapped, and then burst.

She came apart, shuddering, and crying into his mouth at the agonizing explosion. She gyrated against the beautiful waves that pummelled her.

It was *good. So good.*

He kept kissing her. Kept moving and thrusting, sending JJ into her pleasure. Shudders rocked her and love caressed her. Tremors ripped her apart and his groans made love to her as he reached his climax.

After awhile, the savage shudders ebbed away, leaving them wet with perspiration and their breaths echoed fast and furious throughout the dark room.

"Wanna sleep? he muttered a long time after they'd quietened. He stayed within her, his cock impaling her, as he rolled them both back onto their sides.

"Never," she heard herself mutter.

She held him tighter and then she slept.

Rafe grinned and closed his eyes. He listened to the lullaby of her breathing as it mingled with the faraway hoots of an owl. Somewhere in the house he thought he heard one of the guys moan as one or both masturbated themselves to sleep tonight, just as he'd done many nights while listening to Brady or Dan making love to her on each of their nights. He felt sorry for Brady and Dan not having JJ in their bed tonight, but his sympathy did not last for long.

Tonight, she belonged to him and having her lying here with him made him the happiest man alive.

Chapter Two

"SHE LOOKS DIFFERENT," Rafe muttered beneath his breath.

He stood at the stall entrance and kept a close eye on an older cow who had nestled herself on a bunch of straw. Her pain-filled bright brown eyes stared back at Rafe, most likely telling him to get lost because she didn't need an audience. She was ready to give birth and he was waiting to see if she would need a helping hand.

Overhead, rain pummelled the barn roof and slapped against the window panes. Thunder boomed somewhere south of the lake.

Today had turned out to be a washout with the weather, so they'd kept themselves busy in the barn with work.

Rafe had been thinking about JJ since he and Dan had returned yesterday. There was something different about her and he hadn't been able to pinpoint exactly what.

From nearby, Dan set the shovel against the wheel barrel where he'd been heaving cow manure from one the empty stalls. He chucked off his gloves and met Rafe by the stall door.

Suddenly the Angus mooed her distress.

"She looks okay to me. She's doing great," Dan said as he peered into the stall.

"Not the cow. I mean JJ," Rafe said in a lowered voice. He didn't want Brady to hear. He was standing at the workbench repairing a pitchfork handle that had snapped in two a couple of days back.

Dan frowned.

"What do you mean?" he asked.

"Something is up with her."

Dan swore softly and then grimaced.

"What? Like another secret? The last time she had a secret, she was flying planes without telling us. Although I didn't show visual distress at that, I've had many sleepless nights worrying about her flying solo. I don't think my heart can take another secret like that."

At any other time Rafe would have laughed at Dan's comment. But not today. Something was seriously different about her.

"I mean her looks. Sometimes she looks as pale as a ghost. I found her in the main floor bathroom this morning. She was tossing water on her face."

Dan frowned. "She always washes her face in the morning."

"I don't know. Just like yesterday she took off into the bathroom so fast, saying she was air sick. She never gets air sick."

"She's always been a bit on the pale side. And thin side. And it was pretty windy yesterday..." Dan hesitated.

Rafe turned to look at him. There was a weird look on his face that sent Rafe's stomach into a not-so-nice somersault.

"What?" he asked. He wasn't sure he wanted to hear what Dan thought might be up with her.

"She does seem a little more...plump," Dan said.

Rafe felt his eyes widen in surprise. In a split second, understanding rolled over him in one tumultuous wave.

"She'd tell us if she was..."

"She would tell you if she was what?"

Rafe tensed as Brady's voice boomed from right behind them. Hell, he hadn't even heard the guy walk up.

Rafe glanced at Dan who shrugged his shoulders.

"Might as well tell him, unless he knows something already?" Dan proposed.

"What do I know?" Brady asked with a curious smile. It didn't take a brain surgeon to figure out Brady probably was clueless to any secrets JJ might be hiding. Or he had a damned good poker face because if he knew something, he wasn't letting on.

"JJ and how nice she's been looking lately," Rafe offered.

"What do you mean lately? She always looks nice," Brady replied.

Rafe noticed the slightest furrow between Brady's eyes as his brows dropped.

Man, Brady wasn't kidding? He really hadn't noticed anything different about JJ? The man *was* the only one not wearing a condom with her.

"She's looking like she might be—ompf," Dan said as Rafe gave him a quick kick to his ankle.

"What the hell is with you two? You're both acting weird. I don't have time to play right now," Brady said with a shake to his head. Then he turned and headed back to the workbench.

They stared after Brady. When he began hammering on some wood, Dan made a funny face and whispered low enough so just the two of them heard.

"He'll have to make plenty of play time when the little ones come along."

Rafe chuckled and then let himself into the stall with the mooing cow. It was time to check on this mother-to-be and think about ways on how to find out from JJ if she might be pregnant.

Brady swallowed back as a wave of intense uneasiness swooped over him. He could barely hold the hammer as he banged a nail into a piece of wood that he had no idea what he would be using it for. He just didn't want the guys to discover how shaken he was at what he instinctively *knew* Dan had been about to say.

He'd overheard Dan say the word plump as he'd approached them. Then there had been mention of JJ's looks and the instant Rafe had hit Dan to cut him off, the idea that JJ might be pregnant had slammed into Brady.

She *did* look different now that the guys mentioned it. Sometimes there was a nice glow to her face and yet other times she looked a bit pale and sick. Then there had been yesterday when she'd practically run to the bathroom.

Oh man, she *would* tell him if she was pregnant. Wouldn't she? They'd been trying since she'd asked him right after the cattle roundup this past fall. It had just felt right and natural that he give her a baby. Until that night when she'd asked him to father her child, he hadn't really given such a serious step too much thought.

A baby or two or three with JJ would be something he would just accept. He loved her. He had no doubts about their relationship. Had no jealousy that some day she might want a kid or kids by Dan or Rafe.

Had he still been living in the city; he probably would be straight-laced and stick with a monogamous relationship. But living out here, in the middle of nowhere, there were no constraints.

He just acted on his instincts. He was free to live life as he chose. He knew he would never go back to the city. Would never want the tether of a boring day job ever again. Who needed a white-picket fence in front of the townhouse?

He had this ranch. He had JJ and he had the guys who would take care of JJ if something bad ever happened to him. This life was freedom.

He smiled as the rush of uneasiness quickly faded. Yeah, making a baby with JJ was a good thing. He just hadn't really wrapped his head around the fact that the time might have come for her to be pregnant.

Shit! Had he been in denial?

He blew out a breath and whacked the board a few more times for good measure. Just because he didn't know what the hell he was doing with this piece of wood, didn't mean he wanted the other two guys to figure it out either. Now, he just needed to find out if JJ was pregnant or not. He couldn't come right out and ask her. Could he?

Brady shook his head. No, he would wait until she came to him with the news. Until then, he had a ranch to run.

JJ's heart crashed against her chest as she stepped into the small airport pharmacy. She'd done some research on the Internet the other day about pregnancies and learned there could be a possibility that she might be pregnant even if she had a period. Since discovering that tidbit of information, she'd been a nervous wreck. She'd never been one to have a normal monthly period. It had always been light. A couple of days. The women in prison had been envious.

She frowned as she stopped in front of the shelf containing pregnancy test kits. There were so many to choose from. Which one should she pick?

"JJ! Oh wow! It is you! Long time no see!"

JJ jumped as Kelly came walking down the aisle toward her. Kelly was a pilot who worked for North Country Air. She'd been the one who'd transported JJ to Moose Ranch to start her life there, over a year ago. She'd also helped JJ with her anxiety issues. JJ liked her and enjoyed her company. But not now! Not when JJ was standing right here in front of the pregnancy kits!

Kelly's blonde hair was pulled back in a pony-tail, her cheeks were red, and her blue eyes sparkled as she suddenly wrapped her arms around JJ and hugged her tight.

"How's it going? I'm so thrilled to see you here." Kelly asked as she pulled away and looked around. She was all smiles. Eager to see JJ's men?

For a split second, JJ was glad the guys hadn't flown in with her on this trip. *Your jealousy is peeking through*, JJ silently chastised herself. But she just couldn't help herself with Kelly. The woman was so sweet and pretty that JJ wondered why she wasn't married yet. Or maybe it wasn't jealousy she felt concerning Kelly? Maybe it was guilt? Someone like Kelly *should* be happy, just like JJ was happy.

"Where are the guys? Did they come along with you? I'd love to say hello." Kelly said as she turned her attention to JJ.

"I'm on a solo trip. We needed an emergency part for one of the tractors." JJ replied.

Kelly's face brightened with surprise.

"Oh wow! You are here by yourself? You've come so far, JJ. And so quickly. You look absolutely glowing. You look so different than when I flew you over to the ranch that first time. Wilderness ranch life really agrees with you. You're not the skinny girl anymore."

JJ managed a smile and tried like crazy to think of a way to get Kelly out of this particular aisle.

"What brings you here? I would have thought you'd be enjoying that new cabin you had built out on your land?" JJ asked.

Kelly had hired some builders to build her a lovely little cabin on a lake an hour away from Moose Ranch and JJ had been meaning to go over to visit but she simply was too busy. Right now, her focus was getting Kelly out of this isle. JJ took a couple of sideway steps up the isle hoping Kelly would follow. She didn't. Instead, she now eyed the exact spot where JJ had been looking.

Kelly made a small *O* with her mouth and then her cheeks went pink and she gazed at JJ with curiosity blazing in her eyes.

"For a friend?" Kelly asked softly.

Wow, she was giving JJ an out. She should just answer yes and be done with it. But she also needed to confide in someone.

"Do you have time for a coffee?" JJ suddenly blurted.

Mixed emotions ran through her. She wasn't sure exactly how much she should tell Kelly. If anything. No one knew that JJ was having sex with three men. No one knew she and Brady were trying for a baby. She'd prefer to keep that to herself. But still, it would be nice to talk to Kelly about things.

"You've got me for two hours. Long enough?" Kelly's sweet smile almost made JJ cry and she had no idea why.

JJ nodded and Kelly hooked her arm with hers and pulled her out of the pharmacy.

"Hmm," Kelly said and then bit her bottom lip as minutes later they sat in the airport restaurant, at a secluded corner booth, nursing steaming cups of coffee.

"When a woman is pregnant, she no longer has a period," Kelly continued in a low voice. "But yes, I have heard a woman can still bleed vaginally while she is pregnant."

JJ's tummy hollowed out in a twisting feeling. Now she had Kelly confirming stuff she'd read on the Internet. So, it must be true. She *might* actually be pregnant? Now that the time had come, she wasn't sure if she was happy that may be pregnant? Or sad because she hadn't even realized that she actually might be.

"So exactly how far along are you?" Kelly asked.

"I don't know. I mean, I'm not sure if I am. I thought they were just periods."

"Well you told me you have had nausea. You could count that as morning sickness. It can start already within weeks of you getting pregnant. Are you showing?"

"Showing?" JJ blinked at that question.

"Getting a baby bump? I've heard that sometimes women can tell at four months."

Four months!! Could she be *that* far along?

"You should take that pregnancy test. In fact, you need to get your doctor to confirm it. You need a thorough exam. Bleeding can be from different reasons. Infection or rough sex or who knows."

Fear shot through JJ.

"I could be miscarrying?"

Kelly shook her head and her eyes twinkled with a reassuring smile.

"No, no, I'm sure you're fine. You said you don't have any pain. But you need to see your doctor to rule out anything like an infection or something else that could be serious. And, also if you are pregnant, you'll need pre-natal care, right?"

"I don't have a doctor." Where in the world was she going to find a doctor? She lived in the wilderness for heaven's sake.

"Listen, I know a doctor right here in Thunder Bay that is accepting new patients. She's actually my doctor. Why don't I phone her and we can make an appointment with her? We mention about the light bleeding that you've had for a day over the last three months and I'm sure she'll make you a priority. In the meantime, we'll get you an over-the-counter pregnancy test?"

JJ's heart hammered so hard against her chest, she thought she might actually pass out. This was all so overwhelming. She might be pregnant, yet there might already be a complication? She watched numbly as Kelly quickly punched in a number on her cellphone.

Oh my God. This was all happening so fast. Maybe it hadn't been such a good idea wanting to have her own baby? Especially with all her anxiety issues.

JJ reached for her coffee. Her hands shook so bad she could barely hold the mug. What kind of a mother would she make if she freaked out at everything? What had she been thinking bringing a baby into this world when there wasn't even a hospital nearby in case of emergencies?

Okay, just relax. Breathe. Just breathe. Everything is going to be okay. Just breathe.

The roar of an incoming plane had Brady hurrying from the barn where he'd just helped two first-time mother cows give birth. They'd gone into labour within an hour of each other and he'd been hopping back and forth from one stall to the other like a worrying mother hen. But in the end, both mothers had done a great job and Brady had left them happily licking their own respective calves.

JJ's timing was perfect, he thought as he sauntered into the yard. He was finished for the day and he couldn't wait to see her. He'd already come to the conclusion that he would just come right out and ask her if she was pregnant. He would do it tonight. When they were snuggled into bed together.

Tonight, would be the perfect opportunity because Rafe and Dan would be away for a few days clearing a section for that new cabin they would be building. Brady started down the trail when he stopped abruptly as a rush of panic whipped through him. As he gazed past the straggly pine trees that flanked the trail, he didn't see JJ's white float plane moored at the dock. Instead, it was a familiar brilliant blue float plane.

Worry pummelled him. Had something happened to JJ? Was Blue coming with bad news?

Just as quickly as it had come, his panic crumbled when he spied Blue climbing out of the plane. She was followed by three men.

Thank God! Blue had probably dropped by as a pit stop. Maybe she was low on fuel or wanted to show her passengers the ranch.

Man, he really needed to stop worrying about JJ. She had plenty of flying time under her belt now. She appeared eager and confident with the plane. But still, he always had an uneasy feeling when she went up.

Brady sighed and then he started down the trail toward Blue and her passengers.

The air smelled of pine as he walked, and he noticed how pristine blue the lake appeared today. Bright white sparkles twinkled off the gentle waves and there was not a cloud in the sky. From nearby came a cracking sound of a woodpecker snapping its beak against a tree and as Brady drew closer to the dock, he heard the three men laughing with Blue.

She was a nice woman. Cheerful and friendly. She had a daughter who had been born right here at the ranch over a year ago. It had been an emergency landing out on the ice. JJ had only been here a short time, but she had wound her way into their hearts really fast.

Sometimes he wondered where Blue actually came from. She was secretive about her past, aside from revealing she'd once been a cop and a nurse. People hiding their pasts wasn't unusual up here in the desolate wilderness. Some folks came to search for peace from their demons. Others came for the peace and beauty, yet others, like Rafe, Dan and himself, just wanted to carve out a cattle business of their own and get away from the city life.

As Brady drew closer to the three men and Blue, he noted something familiar about two of the men. A moment later, he realized why.

His younger brother, Mitch! And Paul, his best friend!

"Well, shit! Here's my old brother!" Mitch shouted when he spied Brady.

Mitch's deeply tanned face split into one of warmth and joy as his brother rushed up the dock to meet him. In a second, Brady was being crushed inside a warm embrace.

"We finally got around to coming over," Mitch said as he broke the hug and slapped Brady on his shoulder. Then Mitch stepped aside so that Paul could gave him a quick hug too. There was a third man who joined them. He had a stern look, remained silent and nodded.

Brady returned his nod.

"What the hell are you guys doing here? On vacation?" Brady asked.

"We're neighbours, actually," Mitch chuckled. He pointed southeast of the lake.

"We have a ranch on one of the many rivers that comes off this lake. The one they call Snowy Creek. It leads out to Snowy Lake which is big enough to land a float plane."

Confusion hit Brady. He knew there were a bunch of rivers and creeks at the south boundary of this lake, but he hadn't realized there was a ranch nearby.

"What? Like you're on a wilderness trip or something?" Brady asked.

"Nope, the three of us are Snowy Creek Ranch. We've leased several hundred acres of land from the Canadian government. We're building a spa retreat for race horses. Having fresh air, loads of space to run free and having organic feed for race horses during their downtime is of high demand. And you've said how much you like it out here, so we figured hell, let's join Brady and his buddies. Give them some company."

Truly Brady had no idea how to react. This was just one hell of a big surprise.

"You're welcome to stay here until you get situated," Brady said, suddenly remembering his manners. Although they only had one guest room, he was sure they could figure out something. Brady could bunk with Dan or Rafe and that would free up another room. One of these guys could share that room.

"We've actually already got a camp set up. We've been out there since the snow was gone. Blue flew supplies in for us today and I mentioned I was your brother so she insisted we come over today so we could touch base," Mitch said.

He looked around and frowned.

"Nice place but it sounds kind of quiet."

"I guess JJ is out with the plane." Blue remarked as she joined them.

Brady nodded. "She went into the city. Rafe and Dan are away getting some land ready for a cabin we're going to build so we can use it during fall round-up."

"Paul and I can give you a hand in building that cabin. Daegen can stay back and keep an eye on our place. Right, Daegen?" Mitch said.

The man who'd remained silent up until now nodded.

"No problem," he said.

"Appreciate it. We can use all the help we can get. We're starting at the beginning of August. Show up here and we'll put you to work"

Brady turned to face the stranger.

"And since my rude brother isn't introducing us, I'm Brady, Mitch's oldest brother."

"Daegen," the man replied with a nod.

Brady reached out and Daegen stared at Brady's hand as if it were a foreign object. Reluctantly he reached out and shook hands. The man's handshake was firm and steady, and the dark brooding look on

Daegen's face suddenly disappeared. Brady immediately liked the man. But instincts made Brady believe the guy had somehow been wounded or wronged in some way and was realizing Brady could be trusted.

"Daegen is a man of few words. He was in the military and now he prefers the quiet nature instead of the racket caused by flying bullets," Mitch said. His brother didn't go further into detail and Brady didn't want to pry. Besides, it wasn't his business. Daegen was just another person who appeared to want to disappear from civilization.

"So, you're serious? You've moved up here?" he asked as he turned his attention back to Mitch. He just couldn't believe that Mitch had walked away from his lucrative accounting firm in Mississauga and Paul had left his veterinarian practice there as well.

"Yep," his brother's brown eyes sparkled with happiness. Besides having a really nice tan on his face and arms, his cheeks were red from the fresh air. Brady hadn't seen Mitch this happy since they were kids.

The last time Brady had seen Mitch was a couple of years back when he'd come here for an impromptu visit. He'd been pale and unhappy. When Brady had prodded him asking what was wrong, Mitch had brushed him off, saying everything was fine.

It hadn't been, but Brady knew his brother. He was one stubborn son of a bitch and pestering Mitch had gotten Brady nowhere.

"Come on up to the house. I'll put on some coffee and JJ has a damned good chocolate cake ready to carve up. She made it last night," Brady said.

The men shook their heads.

"We'll take a rain check. Daylight is burning. We have supplies to unload so we need to get back before it gets dark. We have a cell phone, but signals are sporadic. Texting might work. Or drop by anytime. We'll make sure we're here beginning of August."

Wow. This was all dropping on him like a bomb. But in a really cool way.

"Thanks. You guys don't know how much help you'll be. We'll head over to check out your place on our first available day off. But it might take some time. Probably after the final cattle roundup late autumn," Brady replied.

As they slowly walked along the deck toward the plane, Mitch and Brady did a fast catch up on other family members while Blue, Daegen and Paul climbed into the moored plane.

Then Mitch was gone.

A few minutes later, Brady watched the blue float plane as it roared over the sparkling waves. The plane lifted off the lake and then sailed up into the sky. Before long, it became a dark speck and then disappeared over the southeast treeline at the other side of the lake.

Brady shook his head. Wow had that just happened? Had Mitch and the others just been here? It was unbelievable. His brother was starting a horse ranch? Man, it was so cool. They had neighbors. JJ was going to be happy and he couldn't wait for her to meet his brother.

Brady glanced at his watch. JJ would be coming home soon. He needed to get supper started for her.

Unbelievable. His brother was living practically next door. Up here, twenty miles away was pretty much right on the ranch's doorstep. Brady gave out a loud whoop, turned and headed back along the trail toward the ranch house.

Chapter Three

JJ COULDN'T STOP TREMBLING as she glided her float plane over the wavy waters and then arrowed toward the dock. Twilight had descended and thankfully Brady had left the dock lights on allowing her to see where she was going.

Everything had happened so quickly after Kelly had gotten off the phone with the doctor's office. They had asked her to come in right away as they had an afternoon cancellation and Kelly, bless her heart, had taken the rest of her day off, to accompany JJ.

It had felt nice to have someone, other than the guys, to confide in. She loved her three sexy cowboys with all her heart, but sometimes a woman needed to have female companionship.

Living out on the wilderness ranch, it was rare to see another woman. Before she'd gotten her pilot licence, she'd been able to chat with the women pilots who'd drop off supplies for the ranch, but now JJ was the ranch's sole transporter of goods.

Meeting Kelly in that pharmacy had been fate, she thought, as she tossed the ropes out the doorway. She heard them smack against the dock as they fell onto the wood. Quickly, she ducked beneath the plane's wings, and climbed onto the dock. In moments, she had the plane secured.

As she'd circled the lake to come down for a landing, she'd spied the buttery glow of lights spilling from the windows of the ranch. Brady was home. Now she just had to figure out how she was going to break the news that she'd gotten from her new doctor. And she needed to tell the guys too.

JJ blew out a tense breath and turned to gaze out across the lake. Everything looked calm tonight. The sky had turned dark, and there was a quarter moon. The pine trees that hugged the nearby shoreline were black.

She heard little splashes of fish jumping from the water to catch mosquitoes. She knew that one of these days they'd have to squeeze some serious fishing into their schedule to replenish their fish stock. She'd heard that organic fish was good nutrition for pregnant women.

She smiled, swept a hand over her belly, closed her eyes and listened to the sounds of the wilderness.

A song bird chirped from somewhere nearby as it readied itself for the night. Waves gently lapped against the aluminum pontoons of her plane and a loon cried a lonesome melody out on the lake.

It was incredibly peaceful here and she was glad to be away from the city sounds of cars honking, people talking and the ear-shattering roar of plane engines at the airport.

The early June air was mild as it breathed against her and the scent of pine made her inhale deeply. This is where she belonged. This is where she would raise her children.

Happiness spilled through her. She blew out her breath and opened her eyes. It was time to get some of the supplies that she'd bought out of the plane.

She turned and for a split second she tensed as she spied the silhouette of a man standing in front of her not more than twenty feet away. Then she relaxed as she spied Brady's white teeth flash beneath the moonlight. He heart began a strong thump as she noticed he wore his cowboy hat.

Damn her weakness for cowboy hats. She wanted him to make love to her, right here and now, but the plane needed to be unloaded.

"So glad to be back, Brady," She was so glad to see him too and it felt as if her happiness was going to bust right out of her.

"Hey babe, I didn't mean to scare you. You look so peaceful standing there. I didn't want to interrupt."

"I've got a ton of stuff I picked up for us while I was in the city," she said.

Eagerness scrambled through her and she stepped toward the plane.

But he stopped her, grabbing her by her elbow.

"Hold on, beautiful," he murmured as he pulled her around to face him.

She gazed into his eyes and to her surprise, she saw a flicker of worry, but that quickly disappeared and then she saw so much sparkling love.

Emotions burst through her. There was wonder and disbelief and immense love. Sometimes she just couldn't believe this big man loved her.

"What's wrong? Did something happen when I was gone?" she whispered. She fought a slice of anxiety that maybe something had happened to one of the guys.

He shook his head and relief poured through her.

"Nothing but good stuff. I'll tell you about it, later. Much later."

He dropped his hand from her elbow, slipped his palms against hers and intertwined their fingers.

"Shhh, let me just look at you. Do you know how much I missed you, Jennifer Jane?"

She trembled beneath his lusty look. She knew he would show her just how much he loved her when they climbed into bed tonight.

"I was only gone for a few hours, Brady," she teased. She treasured when he got serious like this. It meant he truly cared for her. Truly loved her. It felt so good knowing she was surrounded by such love.

It helped to chase away some of her lingering anxieties and helped her to feel stronger knowing she had his support no matter what.

"A few hours without you is like a lifetime, baby."

Her breath halted as his head dipped toward her. She closed her eyes and whimpered at the explosion of sensations whipping through her as his hot mouth melted over hers.

Oh dear. She got the feeling Brady wouldn't be interested in seeing all the things she'd bought while she'd been in the city today. Suddenly she didn't care about them either. Suddenly she had something much better to do.

As his mouth slid over hers, she began to unbutton his shirt. She wanted Brady. Right here. Right now, on this dock.

"Someone's in a hurry," he chuckled against her mouth. But he began to undress her too.

"Make love to me, Brady," she whispered as she tugged off his shirt and ran her hands over his quivering chest muscles. Gosh, she loved the heat of his flesh. The fresh smell of his body.

"Maybe we should take it indoors?" he asked. But she knew they would never make it.

The fire raging was too hot. He had already removed her shirt and he was working on his jeans. Reluctantly, she slid her hands from his chest and eagerly slipped her fingers beneath the waistband of her pants.

A moment later, they were completely naked. She nestled her hands on his waist hoping he would simply thrust into her. He didn't.

Warm lake air breathed against her body as he kissed her again. His mouth felt like a volcano and his tongue was like a fiery bolt of lightening as it clashed with her tongue.

Brady's hands settled on her hips and he groaned as his stiff cock found and then massaged her sensitive clitoris.

She moaned as pleasure sparked. He growled in response and then he broke the kiss. He popped off his cowboy hat, lowered his head and sucked a nipple into his mouth. Her flesh was tender, and she jerked as his teeth scraped and then his tongue rubbed.

Sensations whirled around her, leaving her panting and gasping. He moved his mouth to her other breast. Pleasure whipped through her as he nibbled and bit.

He sucked until she burned. Then without warning, he let go of her trembling flesh.

His lips melded over hers again and he pistoned into her. She cried into his mouth as pleasure tore through her. She came apart, jerking and moaning and loving his thrusts.

This was perfect. He was perfect. He was exactly what she needed tonight.

Brady was usually a pretty light sleeper. But last night after he'd made love several times to JJ., he'd fallen into the deepest sleep he'd ever experienced. He dreamed of white wolves with gleaming white fangs chasing him through the meadows of their ranch. He saw JJ flying her plane through glittering rainbows and then a giant raven flew into the plane's engine making it sputter. Then JJ was screaming as the plane went down into the forest. He heard a shattering bang and a brilliant burst of orange flames rocketed skyward.

Brady came awake on a gasp, the feeling of foreboding following him out of his dream. His heart crashed like battering rams against his chest and cold sweat blistered across his forehead.

Pristine silence split the air. It was a total contrast to the nightmare he'd just experienced. Beside him, JJ slept peacefully, totally oblivious of his fears for her safety. He inhaled deeply and wiped a shaky hand across the stubble on his chin.

Man! That nightmare had felt so weird. So real.

He gazed over at his alarm clock. Six o'clock. It was time to get his ass in gear. There were pregnant cattle to be fed. Calves to be delivered and a bunch of other chores to do. But first he needed to grab a shower.

As quietly as he could, Brady slipped out of bed, grabbed a fresh pair of clothing, and headed across the hall to grab a shower.

JJ was humming in the kitchen frying up some bacon and eggs for breakfast when Brady strolled into the kitchen following his shower. Oh, she could already smell his clean scent and smiled when a moment later he leaned over her shoulder and kissed her cheek.

"Morning sweetness," he whispered.

"Good morning. How'd you sleep?" she asked as she slid the eggs onto two plates and forked some bacon for each of them.

Bacon was a rare treat for them. Usually they ate fried bear meat or steaks with their eggs. But this morning was a special occasion.

"Okay," he muttered. He poured black coffee into a mug and sat down at the table.

She'd noticed he'd tossed and turned last night. He'd woken her up a couple of times with a couple of moans, but she'd opted to let him sleep, since they'd gone to bed so late.

"How about you? You looked really peaceful when I left for the shower. I tried to be quiet so I wouldn't wake you."

JJ grinned as she slid two pieces of toast onto his plate and set it out in front of him.

"Late nights will do that, and I just woke up on my own when your side of the bed got cold. I hope we can have a repeat performance of last night, tonight?" she hinted, already wishing it was evening again.

Brady chuckled. "Woman, you'll be the death of me."

He grabbed his fork and JJ watched as he dug into his eggs. He brought his fork half-way up to his mouth when he suddenly frowned and stopped.

"What's that?" he asked as he finally spied the item she'd placed beside the jar of homemade rhubarb jam.

"What?" she whispered. She hoped he was going to like the surprise. After all, they had been trying for several months now.

She watched his Adams apple bob as he swallowed. Could see his eyes move as he read the little inscription on the silver spoon. She'd bought the little spoon and had it engraved with a cute saying along with a couple of small feet.

"What does it say?" she prodded.

"We're Expecting."

He looked up at her. His mouth had dropped open as the words suddenly seemed to register. He looked shocked and appeared a little pale.

Oh dear. Maybe this had been a bad idea? Maybe she should have popped the surprise after breakfast? Or when Rafe and Dan had been here? In case Brady fainted?

He swore softly. His eyes suddenly twinkled. Tears?

"We're going to have a baby?" he asked. His voice cracked with a hoarseness she'd never heard before.

She held her breath and nodded.

"Oh my God, JJ. We're going to have a baby? Seriously?" He asked. He was smiling now, staring at her in a way she had never seen him look at her before. Like he was dumbstruck or maybe impressed?

The floor creaked as he pushed back his chair and stood.

Wow, he really was a big guy. He let out a big whoop that actually scared her for a second and then his big hands slid around her waist and he was lifting her off the ground with such ease that she felt like a feather as he twirled her around.

She looked down at him and loved the laughter in his eyes. The huge smile plastered across his face. Oh yeah, he was happy. Truly and deliriously happy.

"We're going to have baby, JJ. This is unreal. We were suspecting something was up. But wow, this is still a surprise."

The guys had been talking? They had realized something even before she had suspected?

He kept twirling her as he laughed. She liked when he was happy, but her tummy suddenly wasn't liking what was happening. Queasiness wrapped around her.

Oh no.

"Brady, put me down," she said. She was going to be sick.

He put her down but didn't appear to clue in that she was now really nauseated.

"How did you find out? When? Did you do a pregnancy test? Where is it?"

Too many questions.

She held up her hand and shook her head. Then she rushed out of the kitchen to the bathroom. She made it just in time.

"Morning sickness. Wow, is that ever cool," came Brady's voice a few minutes later as he peeked in through the open bathroom door.

Cool? Oh man. Was he for real?

"Oh baby, is there anything I can do to help?" he asked as he stepped into the room.

She shook her head and flushed the toilet. She turned on the cold water tap and caught him watching her. He was beaming like a proud father, but she wasn't in the mood to be happy at the moment. She felt exhausted and shaky.

"Just go and finish breakfast. Chores are falling behind."

He looked at her as if she were crazy.

"I can't eat. And chores? I just found out I'm going to be a dad and you want me to do chores? Man, woman! We're going to have a baby. I can't believe it. We need to celebrate. We need to do something special."

Oh my gosh, his romantic side was coming out. She couldn't deal with this right now. She needed to pull herself together. This had been the worst nausea attack yet.

"How about you unload all the stuff from the plane? It's a good thing I brought coolers along and packed the perishables in ice."

Brady laughed. "Okay, okay. In a bit. How far along are you?"

"According to Dr. May—"

Shock rocked his features.

"You saw a doctor? When?"

"Yesterday. To make a long story short, Kelly got me in to see her doctor who confirmed with a blood test. There's more to the story, but I'll tell you later all about it. In the meantime, we really need to keep our routine, Brady."

She needed everything to stay the same. She liked her life the way it was now. Especially now that she knew she was pregnant. Routine would hopefully continue to help with her anxiety issues.

"And we're expecting a Christmas baby," she revealed.

She loved the cute way his mouth went into an O shape. She could tell he was mentally calculating how far along she was.

"We're three months pregnant?" he said.

JJ nodded. "I should have realized earlier when my periods appeared different. They were so light. But the doctor said some women have a bit of bleeding in their first trimester and that's why I didn't really clue in until the morning sickness hung around."

Alarm raced through her as his forehead furrowed. "Bleeding, JJ. That shouldn't happen."

"It's okay. The doctor did a thorough exam. She says there is nothing wrong. Everything is okay."

"But bleeding?"

"She said it could have been from rough sex."

He shook his head.

"No more sex then. We can't hurt the baby."

A jolt of panic shot through her. Oh mercy! No more? Since getting pregnant she needed sex. She craved it even more than before she'd gotten pregnant.

She'd had the same concerns about the baby's safety when the doctor had given her the news. Thankfully Dr. May had reassured her that the pregnancy was coming along very nicely.

"She said we're fine for a few more months. It looks like my bleeding has stopped anyway. As we get further along, we can find other ways to..." she let her sentence dangle, suddenly feeling embarrassed at how selfish she was being, but the doctor had said the baby was fine and there wasn't any reason for her not to have sex.

The look of alarm fell away from his face.

"Creative is my middle name. Are you sure we're good? I mean last night. Man, we could have hurt the baby."

"Just to be safe, no more rough sex," she decided. "And don't worry. Last night was perfect."

Brady nodded. He appeared less stressed now.

"I'm going to head out and get the stuff from the plane. You eat breakfast. You're eating for two now, baby mamma." Brady disappeared from the doorway.

Baby mamma.

JJ grinned into the mirror and gazed down at her belly. She wasn't showing a baby bump yet but the doctor said she would be showing really soon.

A moment later, she jumped with fright as Brady let out another whoop from somewhere toward the back of the house.

Man, he had to stop doing that.

Now that Brady knew about the baby, she just needed to figure out a unique way to hint to Rafe and Dan that their suspicions were correct.

The next time Brady met up with JJ was near lunch time. When he'd unloaded the plane and brought the first cargo of items up to the ranch house, JJ had been in the shower. He'd toyed with the idea of going in and joining her, but truth be told, he was concerned for the baby. This would be his kid and he needed to make sure his or her safety was top priority. Even if he and JJ had to settle down on the sex.

Man, they would have to quit with the ménages too. He wondered how that would go over with Dan and Rafe. But hell, it would just make it that much sweeter when it was safe to do so.

When he'd entered the ranch house the second time, JJ had been upstairs. He figured she was cleaning their rooms. She liked to do that in the mornings. The third time, she'd been out watering their newly planted vegetable garden, so he didn't disturb her and he'd put all the food away that she'd purchased.

Afterwards, he'd hustled out to the barn and adjoining corrals to check on the cows. The new mothers and mothers-to-be were now all fed and tended to. The stalls and corrals had been cleaned with fresh laid out hay, and he'd managed to some other things that had needed to be done. Now he was famished.

His mouth watered as he smelled roast beef. One of his favorite dishes. He washed up in the bathroom and a few minutes later he and JJ were seated at the table. Thankfully JJ said she felt pretty good and her stomach had settled. She was eating like a horse and he really enjoyed watching her chow down the food.

When she finally caught on that he was staring at her she stopped eating and grinned at him.

Damn, she had the best smile.

"Stop it, Brady. You're too sexy with that grin on your face."

"I swear you look more and more beautiful with each and every passing day," he admitted. And he was not kidding. She was so cute, he could barely keep himself from hugging her. If he had his way, he'd be doing it all the time.

Her cheeks went a pretty shade of pink and her eyes sparkled. He knew she was still shy about compliments, but hell, he just couldn't help himself.

"My baby mama is the most beautiful woman on Earth," he gushed. Man, he really was turning into one of those Romeo kind of guys. He'd best stop or she'd dump him for someone tougher. Which suddenly reminded him of their visitors yesterday.

"I got news. Totally forgot to tell you," Brady said as he forked some pasta, a bunch of onions and meat into his mouth. Salt and beef flavor burst over his taste buds and he couldn't stop himself from moaning.

Damn, she cooked just as good as his mother had.

"What kind of news? Did the calves drop this morning?" JJ asked between mouthfuls.

Brady shook his head. Calving season was almost over. There were several cows that were close to birth and he figured with his luck they would all go into labor at the same time. It had happened before.

They used artificial insemination mostly in order to have the cows give birth within a certain period in May and June. He just hoped Rafe and Dan would be back by the time the calves dropped so one of them could help. So far, they hadn't brought JJ into that aspect of the business, mainly because she already did so much for them around here. Now with the baby coming, they just might have to hire some extra help for her. He'd have to mention that to the guys when they returned.

"We've got neighbors. Moved in across the lake. My brother, Mitch of all people."

JJ stared at him as if he'd grown horns.

"Okay, it's not April Fools Day. So why are you kidding me? Is he the accountant? The one who is a year younger than you? I remember you once said he would be the last of your family to venture into the wilderness and during his first and last trip here, he was climbing the walls because it was too quiet."

Brady laughed.

"That's the one. It appears he's following in my footsteps. He and his two partners were here yesterday. They flew in with Blue. Stayed for maybe not even half an hour to let me know and then they were eager to head back to their place again. They'll be doing something with horses. They've been there since the snow melted and the ice went out on the lake."

"You're not kidding?"

Brady shook his head. "No. I'm serious."

He could tell in the way JJ's brown eyes flashed with excitement that she liked the news.

"This is great! We'll have family close by."

Yep, she was happy.

Her eyebrows raised and he knew she was about to ask another question.

"Are his partners doctors by chance?" she asked.

"One is a veterinarian, actually. Why?"

"It's always nice to have someone with medical knowledge nearby. In case we run into some sort of emergency. The online first-aid course I took over the winter doesn't make me feel overly confident in my life saving abilities. I mean I can keep someone alive for maybe awhile but we're so far away from help."

Brady had to agree with her. He'd taken first aid courses also in preparation for living here, but sometimes it did bother him that they were so many miles away from a hospital. But he didn't dwell on it. It appeared JJ did.

"They are about a fifteen-minute plane ride. Probably not even that," Brady replied and shoved some more of the delicious roast into his mouth.

"Man, baby mamma, your food always makes love to my taste buds."

JJ's head shot up at his comment and he winked at her. A sweet smile whispered across her lips.

He wanted to kiss her, but that would lead to other things. He realized JJ was right, they had tons of work to do. It was best to stick to a routine.

Tonight though, he'd be really gentle with her. It would kill him, but he needed to be with her. Talk some more about the future and about the baby.

He steered the conversation to that new cabin they would build and that Mitch and Paul were volunteering to pitch in. She was pleased with that news and when they finished eating, he helped her wash the dishes.

He was glad she didn't protest when he said he'd go upstairs and gather the clothing from all the hampers and bring them down so she could get the laundry going. Helping her out made him feel good.

This afternoon he'd get that old tractor repaired too with the part JJ had brought back and then the machine would be ready to cut some hay, which, to their surprise, was growing faster than any other year since they'd been here.

They had planted a variety of seeds in the fields. Different meadows consisted of different qualities of food for the cattle. Nutritional demands varied during their reproductive stages. Depending on the quality of food in each meadow, the cattle were rotated every one to three weeks to prevent overgrazing. The higher quality meadows were reserved for lactating cows, the growing feeder/stocker calves and when a bull needed extra nutrition. They kept all their plantings logged in a book to keep from guessing what had been planted and where.

Brady smiled as he left the ranch house and walked down the slope to the nearby shed where they housed the tractors and other haying equipment. The sun shone bright and warm in the yard, and a cow mooed at him from a nearby pen. He greeted the plump pregnant black Angus by scratching her behind her ears.

"Hey, I'm going to be a dad. You know that?" Pride breathed through Brady as he spoke to the cow. She blinked up at him with big brown eyes and let out a low moo in answer. He chuckled.

Absently he continued to rub her ears. She was one of their many older cows. Her breeding days were over and after her last calf was weened in three months, she would be joining the other cows that were slated for the autumn roundup and market.

Thankfully calving season would soon be over, and they could get on with branding, castrating the little ones, the haying, moving the cattle to other pastures and building that new shelter. Then would come their weaning season, more haying, the autumn cattle round-up and then the breeding season and...their Christmas baby.

His breath backed up as he remembered the night JJ had asked him to be the father to her child. They'd been in the shower together and he'd been surprised at her request. But he'd easily seen himself as a dad and her as a mother to his kid. He hadn't thought about his answer. It had just been a natural yes. It was a new step in their unique ménage relationship with Rafe and Dan.

He still couldn't believe that she would pick him to be the father for her first baby.

Wow. He'd need to start working on names for the kid. He'd have to ask JJ if she knew the sex. He hadn't even thought to ask. He really didn't have a preference. Girl or boy. It didn't matter. As long as the baby was healthy, that was all he wanted.

Without warning the cow suddenly moved her head and nipped him. He cussed as pain sliced through his right forearm. He yanked away his arm before she could do it again.

Damn! He'd been careless and stupid. Daydreaming around cattle, especially ones that were half-wild due to being outdoors most of the time, was a dangerous thing to do.

The bite throbbed and Brady winced at the sight of blood gushing from the wound. He'd need to clean it with soap and water and get some antibiotic cream onto it. The last thing he needed was an infection and a trip into the city to a doctor. He had way too much work to do here.

Shaking his head, he headed off to the barn. They kept a first-aid kit in there as well as one in the house and several others that they carried along with them when riding the trails. When he cleaned the wound, he'd start on fixing the tractor and think on some names for the kid.

Brady chuckled beneath his breath. He wondered if JJ would allow them to name the child some cowboy or cowgirl name. Maybe John like in John Wayne, his favorite western actor. Or maybe Cheyenne for a girl. He'd always liked that name.

Yeah, John or Cheyenne. The news of his becoming a father was all so surreal. But he swore he'd never felt happier in his life. Yes, life was good.

Chapter Four

THE SHOTGUN BLAST FROM right beside Rafe had him cursing as the harsh report sliced through the mid-day silence like a bolt of crackling thunder. Hell, it was worse than thunder and it was right beside his friggin' ear!

Dan grinned and lowered the rifle. If Dan was expecting to get an earful from Rafe, he wouldn't be disappointed.

"You couldn't wait until I was a few feet away from you? You know how I hate loud noises," Rafe complained as he watched three wolves saunter away from the herd of cattle and calves settled in a meadow.

"Had I waited we would have lost the element of surprise," Dan retorted.

They fell silent and watched. The wolves angled toward the wood fence line that had been erected around the pasture to keep the cattle in. At the fence, the wolves got down on their haunches and bellied their way under the barricade and disappeared into the nearby woods.

Rafe watched the young calves in the field and noted that all of them tended to stick by their large mothers. But he also knew at this tender age of between one to two months, the calves were relatively easy prey to predators, especially if the calf wandered away from the protection of the mother and the group.

"May as well do a perimeter check while we're here," Rafe commented.

Dan nodded and followed him. They headed toward the fence where the wolves had just disappeared.

"The wolves are getting used to us. They aren't running scared like they did last year," Rafe commented.

"Yep. They're getting used to our smell. We'll have to find another way to scare them away. Or if it gets bad we might have to try to live trap them and take them on a long trip out of the area."

Rafe inhaled and nodded. "So far we've been lucky. Just a few kills by the pack, but they might acquire the taste for beef."

"Chances are small at that happening. Wolves prefer rodents and there are plenty around. Besides, the cattle are too big for the wolves to take down a cow putting up a big fight. Five hundred to a thousand pounds of beef coming at a small wolf or several wolves, not such good odds for the little guys. The calves unfortunately are another story. We'll just have to start doing more perimeter checks in the pastures where the cows and calves are housed. Most are closer to the ranch, so the distance travelling isn't bad."

Rafe knew Dan spoke the truth. More frequent checks would be the best way to go to be a deterrent. The ranch was making good money with their prime beef. They could afford help.

"Maybe it's time to call up Brady's sister, Jenna, and see if she can send us over some help from that Cowboys Online company she runs?" Rafe suggested.

Dan nodded. "We'll pass that by Brady. Not sure if he trusts her after what she pulled by sending us JJ instead of men as ranch help."

Rafe laughed as he remembered how pissed off Brady had been that cold winter night when North Country Air pilot Kelly had flown in their new helper. The hand had turned out to be a pretty woman and drunk as a skunk after getting into some wine on the plane in order to "calm her nerves".

Personally, he hadn't thought it would work out with a woman because of the seclusion, but hell, he'd been so wrong and was glad he had been too. Very glad.

Suddenly he couldn't wait to see JJ again. It was the same kind of overwhelming need he'd experienced late last summer when he'd had that accident with the axe slicing into his leg and then being incapacitated while waiting for help. He'd thought he'd never see her again and that's when he realized he couldn't live without her.

He missed her whenever he was away from her. When he worked around the ranch, he enjoyed watching her. He liked the sultry way she moved as she hung up the laundry on the outdoor line. It was so sexy to see her arms up like that while she pinned the clothes. That position reminded him of having her in the shower, her arms lifted and tied, with her at his full mercy. It made him want to grab her by the waist and just start making love to her right there out in the open. And he really liked her cooking and loved making love to her.

He blew out a tense breath and tried to push aside his thoughts of JJ by concentrating on his

surroundings. The afternoon sun was bright, the sky cloudless with a mild breeze. This meadow was lush green and of high quality. It was a special meadow, one of many of the same, that had been planted with seeds earlier this spring. The thick blades of grass would meet the nutritional needs of new mothers and the calves.

Other meadows were reserved for the dry cows, their calves already weaned. They also had pastures specifically planted for the weaned calves.

At the fence line, they split up. Rafe going one way and Dan heading the other. The barriers were makeshift. Made to keep the cattle from wandering into the woods and getting lost. Their spread was just too big to make every pasture secure and keep out the predators.

In order to do that they'd have to go barbed wire and that would interfere too much with the wildlife, so they most likely would never go that far. After a good half hour walk, they met up again and started toward their all-terrain vehicles. They still had a couple more pastures to check and then they'd head back to the camp. Tomorrow there was some more clearing to be done and then they'd head back home.

Yeah, he really wanted to have JJ back in his arms again.

"Oh my God. What happened to your arm?" JJ asked as she spied the white bandage wrapped around Brady's tanned forearm. He'd just stepped into the dimly lit bedroom where she'd been settled snugly in his bed eagerly waiting for him to come out of the shower across the hall.

At dinner, he'd been unusually quiet and she wondered if he was still digesting the news about him becoming a father. When she'd prodded him on the subject, he'd smiled and put her heart at ease by asking about her doctor visit and if she knew the sex of the baby. She'd told him no she didn't know, and then he'd fallen quiet again. She hadn't noticed the white gauze bandage around his forearm because he'd been wearing long sleeves, which come to think of it, he must have changed to a long-sleeved shirt sometime during the day, cause he'd been wearing a T-shirt this morning.

Brady frowned and gave her an absent look before gazing down at his injury.

"Oh, this? Nothing. Just got nipped by a cow. I've laced it with antibiotics. Should be okay in a few days."

Concern rushed through her. "A cow bit you? Brady, let me take a look at that."

She made a move to get out of bed, but he smiled at her, waving her to stay in bed.

"Seriously, not a problem," he said with such confidence that her apprehension about the bite disintegrated.

He wore only a pair of briefs and she could easily make out the thick knot of an erection pushing against the thin white material. She trembled with arousal, whipped aside the sheet and comforter from his side of the bed and patted the mattress.

"Come into my lair, if you dare," she teased and wiggled her eyebrows up and down at him.

He chuckled and slipped his fingers beneath the waistband of his briefs. She held her breath as he slid the material over his hips and downward.

Heat flushed through her as his cock sprang free. His erection was in full salute and it looked so yummy she couldn't help but lick her lips as she remembered the times she'd taken his luscious shaft into her mouth.

"The baby..." he said and then he worried his lower lip as if he'd just blurt out his words without intending to.

"Brady," she whispered, loving how much he already cared for their child.

"I told you that the doctor said the baby is fine. Please, don't hold back with me. I need your love. I crave it."

He sat upon the bed, pursed his lips in thought and was silent for a good half-minute as he gazed at the nearest window. Man, he was really frustrating her. What else was wrong?

Before she could ask, he suddenly nodded, lifted his feet onto the bed and covered himself beneath the comforters. To her further frustration he lifted his arms, clasped his fingers together and slipped his hands beneath his neck.

"Do with me what you will, woman," he breathed. The tips of his mouth were curled upward and she giggled. Sometimes he gave her the reigns with their sex life. It was rare, but it happened.

She smiled and didn't waste any time slipping off her pyjama bottoms and her top. Normally she didn't even wear this much to bed, but tonight she'd caught a weird little chill she hadn't been able to shake. But the chill was quickly forgotten as she moved over Brady.

He gazed up at her and her heart sang. Love so rich and raw sparkled in his eyes and she could barely believe he belonged to her. As she pulled aside the comforters she gasped as his cock stood straight up.

"Oh my," she whispered.

"I'm all ready for you."

"You sure are," she giggled. Suddenly she wanted nothing more than to take that juicy looking shaft into her mouth.

His eyes twinkled with approval as she lowered her face toward his penis.

Excitement poured through Brady as she threw him a teasing grin. Man, he was so lucky having JJ in his life and now she was giving him a baby and so much more.

Brady held his breath as she moved her head closer. He clenched his jaw and fists and moaned as she gently pressed her lips upon his cockhead. Her silky hands wrapped around the base of his pulsing shaft and pleasure flames stroked along his swollen length as she licked and lapped a trail of hot fire upon his entire length.

He growled as she gently nipped his flesh evoking sparks of pain and then she dabbed the tender spots with her sweet tongue. He watched with wide eyed appreciation as she opened her mouth and part of his cock disappeared into her. The heat and pressure from her mouth shocked ecstasy through him.

Automatically he tensed.

"You like?" she asked as she pulled her head away.

"You sure know how to make a man feel good," he growled.

She cocked an eyebrow at him and her brown eyes sparkled with mischief.

"Just good? She asked.

His heavily veined shaft jerked near her mouth, begging for more attention.

"Maybe a little better than good," he teased.

The tips of her lips curved upward. She said nothing and he tensed some more as she drew his cockhead into her mouth again. She sucked hard and impulsively he reached up and sifted his hands through her hair, holding her head steady as she began to bob her head allowing his shaft to enter a few inches and then out again.

"Words don't describe this...ah," he couldn't talk anymore as pleasure ripped through him. She was torturing him with her tongue.

His release was nearing at lightning speed. He wrapped his fingers into her silky curls and hoped he wasn't hurting her. He bucked his hips and sucked in frantic breaths as she bobbed.

She slurped and sucked, twisted her hands around his shaft until he was a quivering mess. Her lips squeezed, her teeth nipped, and her tongue stroked his throbbing flesh like a seductive lover.

In and out, he plunged.

When he sensed he might come, it took every ounce of his self control to pull away from her.

"On the bed," he growled. "Hands and knees!"

He hoped she understood what position he needed her to be in for safe sex. During the day, when JJ had been cooking, he'd snuck onto the computer and searched the Internet for safe sex while pregnant.

He wished he could formulate sentences and tell her exactly why he wanted her in the position, but he could barely get a thought together due to his fried brain. He watched as she got onto her knees and hands. He scrambled onto his knees and positioned himself right behind her.

Then he grabbed the base of his swollen shaft.

She moaned as he slowly penetrated her vagina. She was already sopping wet and her muscles clamped tight around him.

Sucking his cock turned her on. It was foreplay for her as well for him. He knew from previous experiences that she would be turned on big time and would need very little stimulation to orgasm.

He withdrew, then plunged into her again. She gasped, called out at his name and her body suddenly trembled as she exploded.

Her velvety muscles spasmed around his flesh, short-circuiting his senses. He pistoned faster and faster, moving in a rhythmic grind until destructive convulsions lashed him.

JJ joined him in her own climax, her pussy muscles squeezing and within seconds his testicles released the pressure.

He came inside her, crying out her name and shuddering so intensely he swore his entire body was being ripped apart.

But in a good way. A really good way.

Afterwards, Brady stayed inside of her. Holding her slightly rounded belly, he gently brought both of them down onto their sides upon the bed. He reached out, grabbed the tangled sheets and comforters and tucked them in around them.

"That was good," she breathed. She snuggled back against him, and he kept his hand over her belly. Over his baby.

Man, *his* baby.

"Only good?" he teased.

She giggled sleepily.

"Before you nod off, have you been thinking about names for the baby?" he asked.

"I have. But I love all of the names I come up with. I doubt the kid would want a string of a hundred or so middle names and no first name."

Brady chuckled. She had a point.

"Have you been thinking of a name?" she asked softly.

He buried his face into her silky hair and inhaled deeply. She smelled so fresh and clean. She'd be the perfect mother.

"Yeah, plenty of names. I think if it is a girl we should give her your mom's first name and my mom's first name as her middle name."

She remained silent for awhile. He wasn't sure if she'd fallen asleep or maybe didn't like the idea and didn't know how to tell him.

"Mary Jane, or M.J. for short? I love it. I truly do. Oh my gosh, why hadn't I thought of that?"

"You would have."

"And if it's a boy?" she asked.

"John after John Wayne."

JJ giggled. "Seriously?"

He cuddled her closer to him.

"Do you know what? We'll name the kid whatever you want, sweetness. Whatever you want is perfect for me. Just like you're perfect for me," he muttered.

"I love you, baby daddy," she whispered.

"I love you too, baby momma."

They slept.

JJ WAS JUST REMOVING supper from the oven when she heard the roar of all-terrain vehicles coming into the yard. Her heart pounded with excitement as she looked out one of the kitchen windows and saw Dan and Rafe on their vehicles, trails of dust-devils following them as they drove up to the vehicle maintenance shed.

They would be hungry and she'd prepared tons of food for them. Quickly she placed the veal stew into a dish and set it upon the table. She'd tried for a baby theme for supper, wondering if the guys would pick up on it and ask questions.

Or as Brady had mentioned the other day, Rafe and Dan had already been suspicious and might guess right away when they spied the miniature sized vegetables she'd picked fresh from the garden only an hour ago.

For dessert, she'd serve her men white chocolate dipped strawberries. They were in the fridge right now.

She'd drizzled some light pink and baby blue-colored chocolate icing over the white chocolate dipped strawberries to add to the baby theme she'd planned for tonight's supper. Brady had loved her idea when she'd asked him earlier after venturing out to the equipment shed, were she'd found him still working on that old tractor that he loved so much.

She'd purchased a bunch of fresh strawberries the other day while in the city because she'd been craving strawberries for weeks. She'd anxiously been waiting for the ones in their garden out behind the ranch house to ripen, but that wouldn't happen until the last week of June or early July, still some weeks away.

Quickly she got the coffee machine going and placed the several groups of baby vegetables onto a large dish. If Rafe and Dan didn't catch on, then she had another type of desert as backup.

Her breath quickened as the back door squeaked open and her men's joyful voices echoed down the hall as they entered the mudroom. She could hear them stop and remove their boots, before coming down the hall.

Rafe entered the kitchen area first. His clothes looked dusty and rumpled, his bangs were wet and his forehead shone with sweat. But that smile on his face made her heart leap with joy. He didn't say a word as he scooped her into his arms. He hugged her and then kissed her ever so sweetly on her mouth.

"Man, you taste damn good," Rafe said with a smile as he let go of her and then held her at arm's length as he allowed his gaze to roam all over her.

"You are a sight for sore eyes, lady," he chuckled.

"Hey, quite hogging her. My turn," Dan growled as he also came into the kitchen.

Rafe chuckled and reluctantly let her go. Then Dan was embracing her. His arms were tight and confident around her waist. He smelled of gasoline and pine. She could hear him inhaling. He was smelling her, she knew, because he often told her how nice she smelled.

"You smell like a flower. Missed you, babe. Glad to be back," he said and let her go.

"Hungry?" she asked as she moved to the coffee pot.

They guys enjoyed their coffee and she loved welcoming them home with as much coffee as they could drink.

"Hungry in more ways than one," Dan said in a soft voice from behind her. "But food first. To make sure I have plenty of energy for later."

Her breath hitched at his remark and she blew out a tense breath. It would be the three of them with her tonight and it would be a fine homecoming.

Brady chuckled from behind the two men and winked at JJ as he accepted the coffee carafe she handed to him. He ushered the guys to sit at their places and then he began pouring their coffee. Before long the three of them began talking about their work days as they always did over dinner.

Brady informed them that the tractor was up and running again, ready for the haying which he planned on starting tomorrow. Rafe and Dan gave the news that the clearing for the log cabin was all set. The logs for the cabin had been cut by chainsaws and ready for use. All they needed to do was fly in the lumber for the roof and frame and a portable generator. They agreed that JJ would be transporting all the needed items with Rafe and Dan tomorrow.

Happiness splashed through her as she took peeks at the guys. They were all so handsome as they ate with ravenous appetite. They were tanned from the outdoors, their faces lined with serious expressions as they listened to each other.

Yep, she did notice that Rafe and Dan hadn't picked up on the baby theme with the vegetables. But they would. Sooner or later. They would.

"Pretty lady, that was the best meal I have ever eaten," Dan said as an hour later he patted his full belly and winked at Brady and Rafe who sat in their respective places on the couch while JJ served up some more coffee to them.

Man, it really felt good to be back home. They'd only been gone a few days and nights and it had felt like a month.

"What exactly did you like the most out of that meal?" Brady suddenly asked.

Dan shrugged. That was an odd question.

"Um everything. Like everything. The baby potatoes were my favorite. How in hell did you get them already from the garden? I mean we just planted a month ago."

"I bought them," JJ said as she breezed back into the living room with a plate of what looked like white-chocolate dipped strawberries.

"You bought potatoes? We have a bunch down in the storage. Why buy potatoes?" Dan frowned. That was a weird thing for JJ to do. She was always pretty frugal about saying they should eat what they had before spending money on food.

"Yeah, JJ. Why buy potatoes when we already have them?" Brady mused.

There was an odd happy tone to his voice tonight and Dan *had* noticed the weird little looks between her and Brady now that he thought about it.

"Maybe she wanted a certain type of potato?" Rafe said as he picked up one of the strawberries and shoved the whole thing into his mouth. His face scrunched up with delight as he chewed.

"Man, these strawberries are good," Rafe commented.

He gazed over at Dan, grabbed another one and popped it into his mouth. A bit of pink juice oozed out of the side of Rafe's mouth as he chewed.

"Well, they do look good. Nicely decorated," Dan replied as he observed the dessert. JJ had gone all out with these strawberries. Each one had been dipped in what he assumed was white chocolate and then drizzled with light blue and light pink lines. He wasn't much for strawberries. Preferred raspberries himself, but what the hell, he may as well try one.

He grabbed a strawberry and took a tentative bite. Sweetness splashed over his taste buds. He moaned at the delicious flavor.

"Wow. Nice," he mumbled as he chewed.

From right beside him, JJ laughed. She had returned to the living room and held another plate in her hand.

"Hey, I know you aren't partial to strawberries, but it sounds like you changed your mind. I guess I'll bring these raspberry cookies back to the kitchen?"

She turned to leave.

"No! Wait! I got plenty of room for both," he urged. He held out his hands for the plate.

"Okay, enjoy," she said as she handed him the plate full of odd-looking cookies.

Odd meaning he'd never noticed her every making square cookies before. They were kind of cute, he thought as he placed the plate onto the coffee table.

She'd decorated them to look like calendars. All of the cookies had a white icing background. The icing lines were blue and pink. Huh, each cookie had an iced heart in one of the squares. Some pink. Some blue. All with the same date. The number 25 on top of the heart in one of the rows and columns and the word December printed in pale blue icing sugar across the top.

"Man, this is alot of intricate work for a cookie," Dan heard Rafe comment as he grabbed a cookie and took a bite.

Dan followed suit. Flavor exploded in his mouth. He tasted the raspberries and yeah, a new love for this delicious icing.

"Outstanding. Really good, JJ," Dan said between chews.

"So, what's the significance of the date?" Rafe asked.

"Yeah, you must have felt Christmassy or something. December 25. Was it so hot here while we were gone that you had to cool down with winter thoughts?" Dan joked.

Rafe laughed. Brady didn't. His face looked stoic.

Dan gazed at JJ. Oh. Oh. She was frowning at them. So was Brady.

Shit. What had he said wrong? He looked over at Rafe who was gazing at the plate of cookies and then looking at the strawberries. He was frowning too.

"What the hell is going on with everyone?" Dan asked with a laugh as he looked from JJ to Brady. Things had suddenly turned way too serious.

He gazed over at Rafe who now had a weird expression that Dan had never seen before.

Okay. What was he missing?

He'd told JJ that he liked the dessert. Told them the cookies looked Christmassy. Well, actually only the date was Christmas. The rest...the rest was decorated in white, pale blue and pale pink.

Come to think of it, they were the same colors as the white-chocolate dipped strawberries. Which, he suddenly wanted another.

He grabbed a strawberry and shoved it into his mouth.

Damn good!

"I'm guessing Dan hasn't caught on," Rafe said with a chuckle. Suddenly there was a huge smile on Rafe's face.

"Let's see how long it takes. Anyone want to take bets?" Brady mused.

He was smiling now too. And so was JJ.

Obviously, the joke was on him.

"What?" he asked, and then squirmed uneasily on the sofa. *What the hell is going on?*

"How many more hints do you think he needs?" Brady asked JJ.

She shrugged.

"I do have one more idea. Hang on," JJ said.

Hints about what? What were they talking about? Why was he the odd man out?

Dan watched as JJ hurried back into the kitchen. From a cupboard, she withdrew three white mugs that he'd never seen before. She smiled and he got uneasy when he noticed tears in her eyes as she handed first a mug to Brady, another to Rafe and then one to himself.

Her voice was soft as she handed him the last mug. He didn't look at the mug. Instead he was looking at her and thinking how absolutely beautiful she looked tonight dressed in her jeans, and pretty white blouse and her usual apron.

Why did she look so radiant?

"I was saving this for tomorrow's breakfast coffee, but since we are in such a dire situation," she said and nodded to the mug in front of him.

Dan gazed at the light blue and light pink writing of the one word written on the white mug. His jaw dropped and his mouth opened with shock.

Daddy.

Shit.

Oh my God.

Reality hit him like a ton of bricks. His head snapped up and suddenly Rafe was up on his feet shaking hands with Brady and then hugging JJ.

"Congratulations!" Rafe shouted.

Dan stood. Noticed he was shaking all over. Man, it finally happened.

"We're going to have a baby?" Dan asked dumbly.

JJ nodded. Tears sparkled like glistening jewels in her pretty brown eyes.

"You guys are going to be daddies," she said softly. She was smiling and Dan thought he had been prepared for this. But wow, this news knocked the wind right out of him.

Suddenly Brady was slapping Dan on the back and JJ was watching him with curiosity. Emotions welled up and damned if he didn't want to freaking cry.

Like, what the hell? He was just so bloody happy for all of them.

"Man, this is cool. Really cool," he muttered. He stepped forward and embraced JJ.

"We're all going to be a family," she whispered into his ear.

Oh man. Family. Dan hugged her tighter. This ménage relationship was really going to be permanent. After the longest hug in their history, he let JJ go and discovered Rafe and Brady watching them with huge smiles.

"Cool news, eh?" Brady asked.

"When did you find out?" Dan wondered out loud. Had Brady known for long? If he had, he had a pretty damned good poker face.

"I just found out day before yesterday and told Brady then," JJ revealed.

"I need more coffee. Who wants more coffee?" Rafe asked. He headed into the kitchen.

Yeah, he needed some too. It was going to be a long night of celebrating because he for one was too wired to sleep tonight.

They were all going to have a baby!

Chapter Five

THE NEXT THREE DAYS passed by like a wonderful dream and JJ swore she couldn't feel any more content. If she would have gotten any happier, she would burst for sure. All the guys were excited about the baby. But even with a baby on the way, chores still needed doing.

She flew Rafe and Dan in with supplies and they returned the same day. The guys kept themselves busy planting seed in the fallow meadows so there would be plenty of hay to cut during the summer and autumn to store in the barn for winter feed.

In the meantime, with her pregnancy came the cravings. Goodness, she craved pickles and sex. Wanted pickles and sex all the time.

It was a good thing Dan was an expert at pickling and canning. Last autumn they'd set aside plenty of preserves from their large garden and she had already made her way through the sweet and sour pickles and was now starting on the dill pickles.

Damned hormones. They would be the death of her yet. Thankfully she had her men to keep her satisfied sexually.

Well, two of them for now.

Early this morning, Brady had taken off for a couple of days to hay the far north pastures which were already producing. He'd left her with Dan and Rafe and they had been out in the barn most of the day keeping busy with the last of the calving. She couldn't wait for them to come inside. Wanted both of them to make love to her.

JJ inhaled softly. She needed to stay in control. She was being silly giving into these cravings. She'd read online that increased cravings for sex did happen to some women. Just her luck that it would happen to her.

She tensed when she heard the mudroom door open and the guys stomp inside. There was a pause and she imagined them removing their boots. Then they walked down the hall, talking, and laughing. Just as she suspected they'd removed their footwear because the clomping sound was gone.

"Hey baby," Rafe said as he strolled into the kitchen. It didn't appear that he noticed she was stirring the pot of vegetable soup because he just grabbed her by the waist and barely gave her enough time to make sure the wood spoon was dropped onto the stove before her feet left the floor.

He lifted her into the air and he laughed as she quickly grabbed his taut shoulders to hold on. It wasn't that she didn't trust him and that he would drop her. It was an instinctive reaction, grabbing him. Her fingers dug into strong muscles and mercy did the feel of his hard flesh make her lower belly quiver with excitement. He brought her closer so that their faces were mere inches apart. His eyes glittered with mischief and his lips parted, anticipating a kiss.

An invisible thread pulled her head forward and she kissed him. Tingles of arousal exploded against her mouth. Rafe groaned. The sound was guttural and primal answering to her own mad desire to mate.

She wondered where Dan had gotten off to. Wondered if he would mind finding Rafe making love to her right here in the kitchen.

Rafe's kiss intensified, rocking her senses. Never mind about Dan. Her arousal was going haywire.

"Make love to me," she whispered as she tore her mouth away from his. Fevered heat coursed through her and her breaths came out in fast pants as Rafe gently placed her feet back upon the floor.

From behind Rafe, Dan chuckled.

"Your wish is our command," Dan growled. JJ opened her eyes and peeked around Rafe to find Dan standing there. He was completely naked, except for the dark brown cowboy hat plopped crooked on his head. His erection was in full bloom.

Yes! Sex time!

"Rafe was the distraction, so I could get out of my clothes," Dan announced.

She giggled. "Supper is almost ready. Aren't you guys hungry?"

She knew instinctively that they would take her meaning in an erotic way. Of course, that *was* her intention.

Dan stepped forward and swept her into his arms. He was breathing heavily as he gazed down at her.

"Another surprise awaits out on the porch," Dan whispered as he carried her out of the ranch house and onto the veranda.

"Oh wow! Were you two guys expecting to sleep outdoors tonight," JJ asked when she spied the nearby picnic table laden with a sleeping pad, pillows and blankets.

She knew what they were up too. Sunset sex.

"A night out under the stars with you would be a dream come true," Dan murmured against her ear. She had expected him to place her on top of the table or at least on her feet, but he didn't.

Instead, he held her tight in his arms and faced her so they could watch the sunset.

The mid-June sky was aglow with red and orange clouds.

"Red in the sky. Probably another storm." Dan said quietly.

They had been getting quite a few of storms, but the guys said it was good. The rain prevented the creeks from drying out and the grass grew taller and lusher than usual giving more hay for the winter months.

A gentle, warm breeze caressed her face as she watched the sun dip behind the darkening forest. Somewhere close by a chipmunk chattered noisily and a cow mooed from inside the barn.

Behind her, the springs of the screen door creaked and she sensed Rafe would be joining them tonight.

"Pretty sight," Rafe said softly.

"She is, isn't she," Dan murmured and nuzzled her ear with his whiskered cheek.

His breathing quickened and she felt his heart pick up speed as it pounded against her arm.

"Anyone want some watermelon?" Rafe asked.

Before she could answer yes, she would love some, a large chunk of the red watermelon flesh appeared before her face.

"Looks yummy," she said. Boy, did she mean it!

She took a big bite and juices sprayed everywhere. Sweetness exploded inside her mouth and she moaned at the wonderful flavor and the cold liquid. As she nibbled on the ultra-large chunk that Rafe held, juices dribbled over her lips, cheeks, down her neck and between her breasts.

"This is delicious," she complimented.

She laughed as Dan licked the juice that had settled at the left corner of her mouth. His hold on her tightened and he brought his head closer. His warm lips intimately brushed her neck, and his tender touch made her quake with anticipation.

Her gaze strayed to Rafe who was now removing his shirt. In the twilight shadows, she spied the hunger tightening his expression.

She caught sight of naked flash. Her eagerness grew.

Muscles rippled across his chest as he tossed his shirt onto the nearby porch swing. She sucked in a breath as Dan leisurely rained seductive kisses across the breadth of her collarbone.

Rafe caught her watching him and he grinned. Oh boy, she loved his cute smile and the flash of his white teeth. His eyes darkened and his jaw flexed as he picked up another chunk of watermelon and poised it against her lips.

She eagerly accepted the sweet treat, sucking it into her mouth, enjoying the wetness splashing over her tongue as she bit and then chewed the delicious dessert.

"I've been waiting all day for tonight. It's a wonder I can get any work done," Rafe growled.

She whimpered as she watched Rafe reach down and remove his pants and underwear. His big cock straightened with lightning speed. Her breath caught at the weave of pulsing blue veins and the angry red flesh that demanded attention.

"You make me so hot when I hear that sound," Rafe confessed as he grabbed the base of his shaft with one hand and stroked the length of his pulsing flesh with his other hand. His penis jerked and thickened.

JJ began to tremble in Dan's arms. The anticipation of having both men taking her was making her wild.

Suddenly Dan stopped kissing her and set her on the edge of the picnic table. His eyes were heavy lidded with lust as he moved aside and allowed Rafe to step in front of her.

She inhaled sharply as Rafe reached out and slid his fingers beneath the waistband of her shorts and panties. She lifted her butt and he slid off her garments.

Then he gripped her ankles, lifted them, and placed her feet wide apart near the edge of the table, fully exposing her lower half to his appreciative gaze.

He licked his lips and JJ just about moaned aloud as she realized what was coming next.

"You're creaming, baby. I mean really creaming. You're going to be a banquet for me. For us."

She whimpered as Rafe dropped to his knees before her and stared between her legs. His calloused hands traveled up along her inner thighs, his hot touch sending her legs to trembling.

JJ jerked as his fingers massaged the outer folds of her pussy. He dipped a finger into her vagina, collecting juices, then caressed her aching clit.

Dan suddenly appeared beside her.

"Let me help you with this," he said as he began to unbutton her blouse. Within seconds, he opened the edges of her top and cupped her sensitive breasts.

"Come on, baby. Lay back and make yourself more comfortable," Dan suggested.

She did as he said and lay down, careful to keep her feet on the picnic table. She settled her head onto a plump pillow and reached up to cup her hands against the back of Dan's neck, drawing him closer. He let one of her breasts go, and then replaced it with his hot mouth. Warm lips melted over her nipple and he sucked.

"Oh that is wonderful," JJ gasped at the erotic pressure.

The feel of Dan's tongue as he flicked gently against her tender left nipple snapped pleasure through her.

With every week that passed, her intimate parts became more and more sensitive.

Between her thighs, Rafe's hot breath caressed her pussy. She cried out as his mouth melted over her clit. She closed her eyes and sank into the pleasure.

She just lay there and adored how their hungry, desperate mouths made her shake involuntarily and increase her need for penetration.

Dan moved his mouth to her other breast. She thrashed about as he circled and licked the areole and then drew her nipple into his mouth and sucked it like it was a lollipop. She shuddered as convulsions rocked into her.

The need for lovemaking grew so strong and so intense, so quickly, she was keening for them to take her.

They ignored her pleas.

Their mouths slurped and licked and made love to her senses and to her body.

Erotic frustration made her keen louder.

Finally, Rafe broke down.

"I'm taking her," he snapped in a guttural growl.

JJ keened her relief. Dan pulled away from her.

The air around her moved as both men quickly changed into new positions.

She arched and gasped as Rafe's thick, hot erection slid into her. Her pussy clenched around the wonderful intrusion and she shuddered as Dan ordered her to open her mouth.

Instincts told her that Dan had climbed onto the table and was now lowering himself over her face.

Opening her mouth, she then accepted his shaft. She tangled her fingers near the base of his erection and held on as Dan started a fast pistoning between her quivering lips. Erotic shudders rocked her as Rafe stretched his penis into her vagina. His shaft was hot and heavy, touching all the aching areas deep inside of her that needed to be loved.

Rafe joined Dan in a fast, yet tender thrusting rhythm. It didn't take long before both men were warning her they were about to come.

But she barely heard them. Tremors of electricity embraced her and swept her away. It was all so wonderful.

Sensations of color and pleasure and sweet pain. They intermingled like a kaleidoscope and burst through her mind in searing ecstasy.

This was so exactly what she needed tonight.

Yes! Yes! Yes!

A rumble of thunder echoed through JJ's sleep and with it came an ominous feeling that something was *seriously* wrong. She didn't know what. Didn't know how she knew, but it had to do with Brady. Shivers and dread snapped through her and she opened her eyes.

Lightning blinked at the windows and snores from Rafe and Dan reverberated through Rafe's bedroom where they'd ended up after an evening of picnic table sex, followed by supper and then another round of hot sex in here.

She snuggled deeper into the blankets and against Rafe and Dan as thunder roared close by.

Her tummy clenched with dread as the phone suddenly rang.

No.

Beside her, Dan grumbled something and she held her breath as he rolled away from her and reached for the phone.

"Moose Ranch," he said in a gravelly, sleepy voice.

He said nothing for a moment, then he sat bolt upright.

Another round of lightning flashes allowed her to see the expression on Dan's face. His eyes were open, his forehead furrowed.

Brady. It had to be. Something is wrong with Brady.

"Yeah, sounds like it. What's the temp?" Dan said in an unusually calm voice.

Temp? As in temperature?

On her other side, Rafe moved and then he sat up too. Any other time she would be loving the way the lightning illuminated the room allowing her to see his muscles ripple across his chest as he scrubbed a hand over his bristled jaw while he yawned, but right now she just couldn't think straight.

"Can you walk?" Dan asked.

Oh my God!

"What's going on?" Rafe asked. She heard him flip the switch on the bedside lamp. Nothing happened. The electricity was out. They'd have to get the generators going.

"I'm not sure what's happening," she whispered. Cold shivers were racing through her and her heart thundered with an ominous sense of anxiety.

"We'll head out right away. Stay lying down and pop some pain killers," he said into the phone.

Pain killers? This was not good. Had Brady injured himself?

Dan hung up.

"It's Brady, isn't it?" she asked. She hoped against hope she was wrong.

Oh, please be wrong.

When he nodded, her hand flew to her mouth to stifle the scream. Fear rocked through her and she thought she might faint.

"We need to get him to a hospital. He suspects lockjaw from a cow bite."

"Lockjaw? Brady didn't think the bite was serious!" she shouted.

How long ago had that bite been? Days ago. Lockjaw was deadly! Why had she allowed him to brush that injury aside so easily. Why had she forgotten about it?

"Aren't his shots up-to-date?" Rafe asked as he hopped out of bed. He padded over to the corner of his bedroom where he kept a battery-operated lantern on his desk. A moment later a dim light lit the bedroom allowing her to make out Dan's facial features. He was pale. He looked...devastated.

"He said he didn't give it much thought when it happened a few days ago. Says he figured the bite wasn't too deep and he'd cleaned it thoroughly with soap and water and has been applying antibiotic cream. Lockjaw only sets in if it doesn't have oxygen to survive so he figured since the bite wasn't deep he was safe. But after waking up and feeling under the weather and having some symptoms that steer him toward lockjaw, he thinks that he might have been overdue for a booster. If he is right and we can get him to a hospital in time, maybe they can do something..."

"Can you fly the plane in a storm?" Dan asked as he turned to JJ.

Automatically she remembered what she'd learned about flying in bad weather. The best thing was not to fly unless an absolute emergency. Her thoughts turned to the frightening flight last year when she and her flight instructor had flown in the dark and landed at daybreak in a small lake to rescue Rafe who'd seriously injured himself and had holed up in one of the many shelters on the ranch. That had been when she'd made up her mind that having their own floatplane was essential.

However, during that rescue trip, she'd had help from another pilot. A very experienced one. But she'd also been doing a lot of flying since then and despite the creepy shivers crawling over like a bunch of spiders at the thought that this would be her first solo storm flight, she knew she could not let Brady down. The plane was the fastest way to get to him.

"JJ? Can you fly in a storm?" Dan asked again. He'd climbed out of bed and was gazing out the rain-streaked window.

"What time is it?" she asked.

"Four-fifteen," Rafe called out as he tugged on a pair of jeans.

"If I can see, then I can get us there," she said with a firm nod. "I need you guys to get the gear, food, first aid kit and maps together and whatever else you think we need and meet me at the plane."

It would be best if they waited out the storm. But Brady was in serious trouble. There was no room for doubt. No time to wait. She had to get to him before it was too late! Or maybe it was already too late?

No! No! She would not let the father of her baby die. No way in hell!

JJ paced her breath as she sped up the plane. Rain pummelled her windshields and the wipers were flying at full blast. But she could see. Barely.

Wind buffeted the plane and lightning flashed high in the grey sky. Thunder boomed. She knew she was being irresponsible going up in this weather, but she really wasn't thinking about herself, her baby or anyone else. She only hoped God understood why she was going up and that he would protect all of them.

Rafe and Dan hadn't asked her anymore questions about the weather and flying. They'd shown up at the plane in record time.

Rafe informed her that he had radioed Brady's brother, Mitch who told Rafe that not only was Paul a veterinarian, he was also trained as a Wilderness Emergency Medical Responder. They had debated on the phone whether they should swing by and pick Paul up and then head over to Brady with him, or cut out the lag time and just go and get Brady and then pick up Paul on the way to the hospital.

She'd been mildly relieved to learn that Paul was a Wilderness Emergency Medical Responder and she wasn't sure the right decision had been made about getting to Brady first without Paul, but she understood that those men would have to get their gear and then paddle through a storm in a canoe up a river to get to the lake for her to pick Paul up. Too many precious minutes would be lost sitting in the lake waiting for them. But if Paul knew something that might help Brady, then getting to Brady first without Paul and medical assistance might kill him. Either way, the scenario was not good.

Bubbles of uncontrollable panic reared and JJ forced herself to stay focused on getting the plane into the air. It was hard. Really hard not to think about Brady. Especially with the guys being so quiet in back.

Too quiet.

A moment later she sighed with relief as the plane lifted off the bumpy waves and into the air. Swiftly she angled the plane toward the northeast. Toward Brady.

Dan replayed what Brady had told him over the phone. His gut twisted at Brady's symptoms. He hoped to heaven Brady was going to be okay. Man, the guy was soon going to become a dad. Nothing could happen to him. Not now.

He gazed out the side window of the plane. The sky looked moody. Bleak. It was getting light and maybe it was just his wishful thinking, but it almost seemed as if the rain wasn't so heavy anymore. However, it was windy as hell. Every few seconds, the plane would shake and his grip on the seat rests tightened.

Up ahead, in the cockpit, JJ was quiet as death. If he was to venture a guess, he'd suspect her anxiety was way over the 1-10 scale. Yet, she flew the plane like a freaking pro. He was so proud of her.

Blades of lightning forked out of the sky, startling him. He suspected if he reached out, he could grab the lightning. Maybe harness the power somehow and get this plane to Brady faster?

He shook his head at that crazy thought. Man, when the phone had rung early this morning, he'd instinctively known something was wrong. No one called this early unless there was an emergency.

Shit! Why the hell hadn't Brady told them he'd been bit by a cow? But JJ had known? She hadn't mentioned anything. She hadn't seemed surprised when he'd told them. But Rafe had been startled. They should have said something about the bite.

Dan bit his bottom lip. Hard. Anger burned through him. Maybe it had been just a nip and Brady hadn't put much mind to it, but still, they could have had a wound looked after by a doctor. Could have checked Brady's medical records or something. They had taken first aid courses and alarm bells should have gone off.

Brady, you damned idiot!

He knew he shouldn't be getting all pissed off. But he was so fucking mad, his head was spinning.

Chapter Six

DESPITE THE CONSTANT rain pummelling the windows and the mist curling around the plane, Rafe was able to spy the lake they were needing to land on and he quickly headed to the cockpit to let JJ know. His heart ached as he found her brushing tears from her cheeks. She'd been crying and flying a plane. He was so proud of her. She was the strongest woman he knew.

"He'll be fine. We just need to get him to the hospital," he said and gently patted her shoulder.

She nodded and angled the plane toward the little lake he pointed to. When he didn't leave the cockpit, she gazed up at him, her eyes full of tears.

She frowned. His gut clenched at all this shit she was going through. Stress was not good for her or the baby.

"You need to get on your seatbelt, Rafe. The descent could get rough. I don't want you flying into the windshield," she warned.

Rafe chuckled. "I think I'd make a nice window ornament for your plane."

To his surprise, she cracked a grin.

"If you don't want to go in back, then strap yourself in here," she replied.

He did as she asked and stared out the windows as the earth began to draw closer and closer. He'd never been one for flying in a small plane, but with JJ at the helm, he wasn't scared. Much.

"If you can get us to the southern most tip, then Dan and I can hoof it through the woods to get Brady," Rafe said as he pointed toward the far end of the lake.

"I'm going with you," she said. Her voice was firm and he knew this was not the time to argue with her, but he needed to set her straight.

"You stay put, JJ. We can't risk anything happening to you. We can move faster without you." He'd expected her to argue but thankfully she didn't. Maybe she'd tuned him out in order to bring down the plane.

His stomach sank in a sickening feeling as she started a steep descent.

"Hey, it stopped raining," Rafe said. He'd suddenly noticed she'd switched off her wipers already.

"It's just a lull. Look off to the south," JJ instructed.

Rafe looked out the front window and noted the dark, ominous clouds rolling in the horizon. Brilliant forks of lightning arrowed through the sky.

He blew out a tense breath. That was exactly the area of the cabin. And Brady. Why couldn't they just catch a break?

Brady groaned as he lay in the bed. He was on his right side, in the fetal position, facing the wall. He'd pulled up his legs and pressed his knees against his sore gut. Everything hurt like hell.

Sweat poured off him. He felt feverish and his heart was beating faster than it should be. His abdominal muscles were stiff and painful. The muscles in his jaw and neck were stiff too and he was having trouble swallowing and breathing. Those were just some of the symptoms he was experiencing.

Every time a crack of thunder snapped through the tiny cabin, the muscles in his body seemed to react to the noise and started a painful spasming that lasted for minutes. The same thing happened when he'd seen lightning flash at the windows. Light just seared into him and made his muscles spasm so bad he hadn't known such intense pain even existed. His senses were in overdrive and he was reacting to everything. He felt so bad...he just wanted to die.

Oh man, he was screwed. He'd never heard of a good ending for someone infected with tetanus. Why the hell hadn't he thought about getting the bite looked after? Why had he brushed it off? He should have listened to JJ and taken it seriously that night she'd found out about it.

But he hadn't wanted to worry her, and he'd cleaned it out so thoroughly and doused it with antibacterial ointment. It had seemed to be healing so nicely, that he'd forgotten about it until last night.

Man, he was glad he'd been able to get through the satellite phone to the ranch. Just hearing Dan's voice had brought him a good amount of relief. Dan had sounded cool as Brady had told him his symptoms and his suspicions. But Brady had been able to detect the underlying current of worry.

He wondered how JJ was holding up? He hoped the guys didn't make her fly in this weather. It was too dangerous. He also instinctively knew if they didn't, he was a goner.

Brady grimaced as another round of spasms snapped through various areas of his body. He'd heard some people infected with tetanus had such bad spasms, their bones would break. Oh boy. If he survived, he just hoped the bones in his arms were okay so he could hold his baby.

A deep well of emotions bubbled up from his chest. He wanted so bad to see his kid. Would it be a girl? Or a boy? As long as the baby was healthy, he didn't care what the sex would be. The kid would be beautiful no matter what because JJ was his or her mother and JJ was gorgeous.

Shit! Why *hadn't* he taken the bite more seriously? Obviously, his tetanus booster hadn't been up-to-date.

He was so damned stupid! Stupid! Stupid!

A noise at the door made him stiffen. Pain gripped his muscles. Everywhere. He winced at the sound of voices. He could hear Dan and then Rafe.

"Oh my God, Brady!"

Oh man, JJ. They'd brought JJ. He didn't want her seeing him like this. He groaned as her gentle hand curled around his spasming shoulder.

"JJ," he managed to whisper.

"You're going to be okay. We've got a litter and we can carry you to the plane." JJ was saying other things but her words seemed to melt into each other. He wasn't sure he understood everything.

"Hurts...like...a...bitch," he muttered. For some insane reason, he wanted them to know it was bad.

"Hang in there, my man. Hang in there," Dan was speaking now.

Pain rocketed through him as hands touched him. He cried out but they didn't leave him alone. He was turned onto his back, then lifted and then down. Then lifted again. He could hear JJ sobbing.

He felt bad for bringing this grief onto her. She didn't need this shit. It wasn't good for her or their baby.

"Hold on, Brady. Hold on. We've got Paul, the vet waiting for us. He knows stuff about tetanus," Rafe said.

He kept talking but once again the words began to mingle, and he couldn't keep track. He kept his eyes closed tight. Felt the cold rain hit his face like painful blades as they left the cabin.

Wind howled. Tree branches cracked ominously overhead. Or maybe it was his bones cracking? His entire body went into spasms again. Fuck! He was going to die! He just knew it.

JJ didn't know how in the world she managed to survive the half hour struggle through the dense forest back to the lake where they'd landed. Dan and Rafe had told her to stay put with the plane, but she couldn't. She needed to be with Brady. Needed to stay with him. She had to be there...in case she had to say goodbye.

Brady looked bad. Pale as a ghost. His body was stiff. His breathing raspy. He was having trouble breathing. She remembered stuff from a first-aid course she'd taken online. About doing a tracheostomy. She would do it if the time came.

She was surprised she hadn't gone into full panic mode and become utterly useless. God help her, but she wanted to, if only to distance herself from this horrible situation. But she needed to keep it together. Needed to stay sane for Brady.

The storm had gotten worse as they made their way through the forest toward the cabin where Brady had been. The wind had shrieked through the treetops. Branches had fallen all around them. The rain was a downpour and the lightning and thunder so intense her teeth had involuntarily chattered.

But they had made it to the old cabin tucked away at the edge of one of the endless meadows on Moose Ranch. She seriously was surprised they hadn't been struck by lightning. Maybe they'd gotten lucky due to all of them wearing rubber boots and raincoats. Or maybe God was listening to her prayers to keep them all safe.

On the way back to the plane, the storm had thankfully passed on.

Now as they waded through the waist high cold lake water, with Rafe and Dan lifting the litter as high as possible to keep Brady dry, her mind once again drew to the possibility she might lose him. If she did, she would probably end up screaming until she went insane.

After they reached the plane, they got a moaning Brady on board and settled him in the aisle on the litter. They'd hurriedly changed into dry clothing, which thankfully Rafe had had the forethought to pack for all of them.

She managed to get the plane into the air without a problem and headed toward the lake to where Mitch would bring that medical responder.

While she flew the plane, tears ran down her cheeks as she listened to Brady moan and cry out. She wanted to be there with him. To somehow soothe his pain, but she was stuck here in the cockpit. Helpless and sick with dread.

When Rafe pointed out the lake where she was to land, she was grateful to see three men waiting along the south shore. As the plane hit the water, the three men were already paddling a canoe out to meet her.

There were hurried introductions as two of the men climbed aboard. She barely noted that Mitch looked a lot like Brady and one of the men, whom she assumed was Paul, had brought along a large black leather bag. The other man remained in the canoe and quickly paddled away from the plane.

She tried to read Paul's face as he kneeled beside a very stiff Brady, but Paul's gaze was expressionless. He swiftly set about his examination and as he did so, he instructed her to get airborne.

The trip to Thunder Bay was the longest and most torturous of her life. The skies had turned a bright blue, sunshine streamed upon the green forest below and white mist uncurled throughout the many lakes that dotted the area, but JJ couldn't revel in the beauty. She was dead inside.

Several times either Rafe or Dan prodded her to eat a sandwich or have some hot coffee that Dan had packed for them. Her tummy heaved at the thought of food or drink, but she knew she couldn't get sick, so she'd forced herself to eat half a beef sandwich and drink a couple of cups of coffee.

One good thing about Paul being on board, Brady wasn't moaning as much. Rafe gave her frequent updates informing her that Paul had already given Brady the tetanus vaccine, had started him on a tetanus antitoxin, and given him a mild sedative to help lessen the muscle spasms. But he couldn't give too much sedation, or it would inhibit Brady's breathing even more.

He'd also started Brady on a strong antibiotic that Paul would normally have needed for the horses they were bringing onto their ranch later in the year.

Paul had told Rafe and Dan he thought the prognosis was serious, but not yet critical. Brady wasn't out of the woods.

JJ prayed harder as the airport came into view. She spied the helicopter on the emergency helicopter pad. She knew the helicopter was there awaiting Brady's arrival because she'd been on the radio with 911 as she'd flown closer to the city giving them her ETA.

Red and blue lights blinked, and the copter's blades were rotating. Medical personnel dressed in white waited nearby with a gurney.

Had the guys not purchased this plane last year, she wondered how they would have managed to get to Brady. Had Brady's brother not decided to set up shop nearby with Paul the vet...She shuddered at what might have happened and tried to concentrate on the air traffic controller's instructions on which runway she was to land.

Once again, she prayed hard. Prayed that she wouldn't lose Brady and that her baby could know his or her father. Angrily, she wiped away the tears that continued streaming down her cheeks. God couldn't be so cruel as to take Brady from them. Please God, not now.

Brady knew the news was bad. The phone call had come early in the morning a couple of days after Christmas. He'd planned on sleeping in really late because he and a couple of guys from the firm had gone out drinking at the local bar. They'd played some pool, chatted with some cute lawyer chicks from a nearby legal aid government firm. He'd even pondered on asking one of ladies, a cute blonde with the prettiest brown eyes, if she wanted to come home with him and spend the night, but he hadn't gotten up the nerve to ask her. He wanted to get to know her a little better before proposing a sleep over with some hot and heavy sex.

A good thing he hadn't asked her because as he'd reached for the phone, he'd instinctively known the news was really bad and the last thing he would have needed to deal with was a woman in his bed that he barely knew.

His sister, Jenna, was on the line. She was crying and muttering something about mom and dad and their youngest sister, Ginny, being in a serious accident. The trio had been on their way up to the family cottage near Huntsville. Dad had been driving, their car had hit some ice on the highway and his dad had lost control.

After a few donuts, the car had stalled. A transport truck loaded with metal rods hadn't been able to stop in time and hit them head-on.

Brady didn't even remember getting dressed. Didn't remember how he got to the hospital.

All he remembered was his brother, Mitch meeting him somewhere inside the front entrance of the hospital, his face ashen, saying Mom and Dad were dead and their sister was in critical condition with a crushed pelvis, a broken hip, head injuries and other broken bones and she wasn't expected to survive.

Mom and Dad were dead. How could this be? How? Or had it all been a dream? Maybe they were all okay?

Brady forced himself to open his eyes. A room he didn't recognize burst into view. The walls were pale green. Hospital room. There was a window beside his bed. Sunshine streamed inside and landed on the lower half of his body. His legs were hot. He tried to move them, but it hurt bad.

Beside him a couple of weird machines whirred softly. He was hooked up to an IV with several bags hanging off the metal hooks.

He tried to swallow. Found it hard to do it, but he managed. Maybe he was the one who'd been in the accident and not his mom and dad and sister? Maybe he'd been in a coma for several months and not his sister?

A burst of panic swept over him. How *long* had he been here? And where was he?

Something warm was curled over his hand and he noticed it was someone else's hand. There was an arm that led to a dark-haired woman. A familiar woman. His heart clenched.

Suddenly things began to fall back into place.

"JJ," he managed to croak.

She was instantly awake. Dark circles hung beneath her eyes. For a moment worry and panic snapped through her brown eyes and then she smiled at him.

Her smile was the most beautiful thing he had ever seen in his life. She squeezed his hand and for some crazy reason his fingers hurt.

"Brady, you are a sight for sore eyes," she whispered.

"Why...you...here?" he rattled. He was surprised she understood because he could barely understand himself. He sounded like a croaking frog.

"Where else would I be, Brady?" she said with a shake to her head. He loved the way her hair bounced. Loved the cute dimples in her cheeks as she smiled some more.

Damn but he'd snagged one gorgeous looking woman.

"The...baby?" he asked. He hoped all this shit hadn't put too much stress on JJ and the baby. *His* baby. What the hell had he been thinking not checking out that cow bite?

"The baby is safe. And yes I have been eating and sleeping and taking care of myself."

He tried to grin, but hell, the muscles in his face hurt. But not at all as painful as when he'd been in the cabin.

"Prognosis?" he muttered. The muscles in his jaw were a bit stiff. May as well know how bad this tetanus shit was going to get.

"Well, the doctors said you probably will have some nerve damage. If so, you'll have some pain in the areas of damage up to a few months until new nerves regenerate. Until then you can take drugs to alleviate symptoms. It was a good thing Paul was there and knew what to do, he saved your life."

Paul.

Yes, he remembered Paul leaning over him telling him he was going to be okay. Getting a couple needles injected into his arm. Things had improved after that.

Things continued to improve as he stared at JJ. Man, she was pretty, despite the dark circles under her eyes. She smelled nice too. Of lavender.

"Does it hurt anywhere?" she suddenly asked.

He nodded and pursed his lips.

She frowned.

He pursed his lips some more and then she smiled. She understood what he wanted.

"Your lips hurt?" she asked softly. Tenderly.

"Big...time," he lied.

His insides went into happy mode as she bent closer. When her warm mouth melted over his, his brain short-circuited and sore muscles in various parts of his body sparkled with pain. But he knew he was going to be all right. And he knew she was all the medicine he would need to recuperate.

Suddenly he couldn't wait to get the hell out of here.

Brady was back on the ranch within a week but confined mostly to the bed or to the couch with limited strolls to the bathroom or to the front porch. On the porch, he sat with JJ while they both folded laundry on the picnic table or prepared vegetables. She loved having him around and they chatted about things he wanted to do with the ranch. He helped her bake and to get food ready for meals and he even made dessert several times.

The muscles in his legs had been affected more than anywhere else on his body. The doctors said he'd been very lucky that he'd gotten prompt attention and JJ thanked God almost hourly for letting her keep Brady. The affected nerves would regenerate, and he should be as good as new within months. But Brady insisted it would be sooner.

While Brady had been in the hospital, she'd gotten to know Brady's brother, Mitch and his friend, Paul. Paul had a friend who also worked at the hospital as a nurse. The elderly lady had been kind to let JJ, Mitch and Paul stay at her small apartment that was near the hospital. They'd stayed there for several nights while the nurse worked the night shift.

Word had come quickly from the doctors that Brady would be okay thanks to Paul's quick thinking of administering the medication he'd had on hand. The strong antibiotics had put a stop to the tetanus causing further damage. So, she'd been able to relax and eat nutritious foods that Mitch and Paul brought to her while she stayed all day with Brady in his hospital room.

Rafe and Dan had returned almost immediately to the ranch via North Country Air along with several months' worth of fuel for the bush plane so they wouldn't have to worry about fuel for awhile. Just because of a serious injury, ranch chores, haying and checking on the cattle still had to be done.

An exciting proposal had been brought up last night at dinner too. Something that made JJ so excited, she hoped it would happen. Brady had suggested they put in a call to Jenna to see if they could send some temporary help thru Cowboys Online. Although Brady was wobbly where his walking was concerned, he told them he was confident that he would be able to help out in building that cabin out near the roundup camp. He suggested they should have someone stay here at the main ranch to tend to the garden, do some haying and keep an eye on the place for a week or so.

At first Rafe and Dan had protested, figuring it was best for Brady that they set aside their cabin plans until next summer, but Brady was adamant. He wanted that cabin built on schedule and he wanted JJ to come along with them.

JJ had suggested they ask Jenna to send Milena, her old cell-mate in prison. She hadn't told them yet about her brief earlier contact with Jenna regarding Milena, and now was a good as time as any. After she'd explained that Milena was in the Cowboys Online program and that Jenna was working on getting her a job, Brady put in the call to his sister. Jenna promised she would call back as soon as possible with an answer.

After dinner, the four of them headed down to the lake, as they had been doing every evening since Brady had come home. Rafe and Dan helped Brady into the water and they walked in until the water hit Brady's waist. Then they walked him back and forth near the shoreline. Brady said the cold water helped to ease the pain he felt when he walked.

JJ plopped down on one of the Adirondack chairs and watched her three cowboys. They wore swimsuits and were bare chested. Muscles rippled in their arms as Rafe and Dan flanked Brady and assisted him in walking.

They were such strong and caring men. And they were hers. Gently, she cradled her growing baby bump. She loved her unborn baby so much that the emotion brought tears to her eyes. She loved the idea that her children would know three very loving fathers and their mother flew airplanes!

Her gaze swept to their float plane moored to the other side of the dock. That plane was a life-saver and she was so glad that the guys had listened to her when she'd suggested to get one for emergencies and for easier transportation on the wilderness ranch. She was thrilled too that they had flown in the drums of fuel through a more experienced pilot earlier this week.

It had been Kelly from North Country Air who'd landed her plane on the nearby landing strip, which was actually just a cleared meadow. From the plane, the drums had been transported via atv and trailer and stored far from the ranch house inside a makeshift wood shed that was equipped with lightning rods.

"Hey, sunshine! Take a look at the sunset," Dan called out. He pointed to the western horizon. Her breath backed up at the array of pinks and blues lacing the billowing white clouds that hung in the baby-blue colored sky. The sun was quickly disappearing behind the forest and dark shadows doused the nearby trees and gently wavy lake.

She stiffened as from somewhere nearby, an owl hooted. The foreboding sound shot a dark chill through her. The ugly feeling of anxiety burst out of nowhere. It happened so fast that JJ was helpless to stop it from taking hold.

Icy tingles slithered through her scalp and fear crept through her. The inner peacefulness she'd been experiencing since finding out Brady was going to be okay, suddenly disintegrated.

Tenseness swept over her like a suffocating cloak as she remembered rushing through the downpour and the forest full of fallen and rotting trees to get to Brady. She'd managed to stuff all her worry deep inside of her over the past couple of weeks and now it was all coming out in one horrible flurry of emotions.

No, not now.

"It looks really nice, doesn't it?" Rafe called out to her.

She nodded jerkily. Her surroundings suddenly felt out of proportion and she just didn't feel right.

Okay you need to calm your breathing. You don't want them to pick up on anything.

Too late. The guys were already staring at her. Assessing her. Knowing she was suddenly different.

Her heart began to pound. Her hands began to shake.

Oh no! This is going to be a bad one.

Calm your breathing.

She couldn't. Her lips began to tingle. Then her hands. She was starting to hyperventilate. She stood. She had to get out of here. Had to run somewhere. But where?

"Easy, JJ," Dan was already beside her.

"Where's Brady?" Panic for his safety snapped through her.

"He's fine. Rafe is helping him. See?" He moved out of the way so she could watch Rafe assist Brady into shallower water. He should be staying in there. He hadn't been in long enough. He said that the cold water eased the nerve pain and he slept better at night after being in the water.

Tears bubbled up. She'd almost lost him.

She started to cry. Everything was so overwhelming.

"You've been through so much, baby. Have a good cry. Come on, let's go up to the ranch and we'll tuck you into bed," Dan said.

She nodded numbly. Wiped away her tears. Her legs trembled as she walked. Dan curled his arm around her waist and held her snug. She felt better. But she still felt as if she wanted to run. To get away. To go anywhere.

"I'm going to need a paper bag, I'm hyperventilating," she whispered to Dan as he ushered her off the dock and onto the trail that led to the ranch house.

"JJ! Are you okay?" Brady called out from behind.

She didn't want Brady to get upset. He'd been through so much. She didn't want him worrying about her.

"Rafe, keep him in the water for awhile longer. I'm fine." Her voice shook. There was no way they couldn't have heard the shakiness, the panic in her voice. They knew she was having an attack.

"Please, tell them to stay in the water. He needs his exercise," she whispered to Dan.

"They're doing as you say. Don't worry," he replied. He walked her faster. They'd left the outside ranch house lights on when they'd gone down to the lake and the buttery glow spilling out of the windows did nothing to relax her.

Her lips and fingers continued to tingle. Her mind raced with "what ifs".

What if Brady had died? What if the baby wasn't going to make it because of all the stress she'd been under lately? What if this anxiety attack never ended?

Once they were in the kitchen, Dan rummaged around in the drawers and found a paper bag. He placed it over her nose and mouth and instructed her to breath. He spoke in low soft whispers in much the same way he talked to a nervous cow about to give birth.

Soon the tingling around her mouth, fingers and hands went away and her anxiety and panic eased. But her heart continued to pound with furious speed. From past experience, she knew the beating would slow soon. She felt exhausted. Shaky. Nervous. Emotional.

"Better?" he asked. He was smiling at her and she needed that right now. Needed reassurance. For someone to tell her everything was going to be okay.

"Any idea what brought this on?" he asked.

She nodded, feeling the emotions rage up again. Helplessness. Fear. The horror of possibly losing Brady.

Suddenly she was telling Dan everything. To her surprise she even blurted her secret worry about something going wrong with the baby.

What if something happened to the baby? If she couldn't fly the plane, they couldn't get to the hospital in time? What if something happened to one of them? She didn't want to lose any of them.

"You're not going to lose us and the baby is fine." Brady's stern voice echoed from behind her.

Oh damn! He hadn't stayed out in the lake.

She was going to screw up his therapy. Another round of hot tears bubbled into her eyes as she saw him hobble toward her.

"Come here," Brady whispered. Tears were in his eyes too.

She walked over to him and he gathered her into his arms. His strength and his warmth poured into her as he held her.

"We're all okay, here. JJ. All of us. We've got Paul the vet who has emergency training. We've got you and the plane for emergencies. You guys all saved my life. We're all a well-oiled machine out here in the wilderness."

"And Paul told me that Daegen knows how to fly too," Rafe added.

Daegen. Of course. The other man who'd been in the canoe.

"So, we're all set. You don't need to worry," Dan said.

"What JJ needs is a heavy-duty vacation. Somewhere where she can relax away from us. Some place she can have massages and get her nails polished and do stuff ladies like to do. Maybe a trip to the Bahamas or something," Rafe said from nearby.

Fury burst through JJ. Not that she didn't want to go to the Bahamas, but because they didn't seem to realize how important they were to her.

She tried to struggle out of Brady's embrace, but he held her tight.

"What I need is my men. You guys are my life. *You* are my vacation," JJ blubbered and pressed her face against his Brady's warm chest. How could they even think of sending her away?

He held her tighter and then she realized he was shaking.

Oh my gosh, she'd upset him?

In a flash, she tore herself from his grasp and looked up at Brady. He wasn't crying! He was laughing!

"You are one feisty woman, sweetness," he soothed. He brushed his thumbs along her cheeks wiping away her tears. His eyes twinkled with amusement.

She smacked him on his shoulder.

Rafe and Dan started to laugh too.

My damn fool awesome men.

"What in the world are you laughing at? Maybe I should go away and then you will appreciate me more," she teased.

The men sobered. Uh huh, they didn't really want her to go away, did they?

She was starting to feel better. Mentally she began to change her way of thinking just as she'd been practicing doing over the winter. She *had* to turn her negative thinking to positive thinking because she didn't want to be stuck feeling anxious at every little thing that went wrong.

What she'd just had was a setback. Setbacks happened when someone was learning something new. She needed to remember that. Just because she'd had an attack, it didn't mean her anxiety and panic attacks were coming back. She had to stay in that mode of positive thinking. Had to get rid of the "what if this happens" and "what if that happens" thinking.

Yeah, easier said than done.

"So, what you're saying is..." Brady grinned as he let his sentence trail.

"What she's saying is we need to find other ways for her to destress," Rafe said with a softness that captured JJ's entire attention.

"Yes, I need to be distracted," she purred with agreement. Boy, they sure did have the right idea.

She hadn't had sex since Brady's illness. She'd been so worried and pre-occupied with keeping him healthy, she hadn't had those naughty cravings. But suddenly those urges were blossoming to life.

"I think we can arrange numerous distractions, sweetheart," Dan said with a wink. "But not tonight. Tonight, you need to relax and have a good night sleep. Then we can talk more in the morning."

"But—"

"No, buts, beautiful," Brady said as he pressed a finger to her mouth. She resisted the urge to lick.

"Come on now, off with you," Rafe said as he grabbed her by her shoulders from behind and steered her to the bottom of the stairs.

"Good night," she said as he let her go.

She smiled at the chorus of good nights that followed her up the stairs. Despite just having had a nasty panic attack, she got the feeling she was going to have a good night sleep.

She was absolutely exhausted!

Chapter Seven

THE NEXT FEW WEEKS flew by as Brady settled into a routine of helping JJ and assisting the guys with the chores wherever possible. His brother, Mitch and one of his partners, Paul the vet, came over a few times to lend a hand and Brady was grateful. But it irked him that his legs were taking so long to get back to how he knew they should be. He could walk but his legs were stiff and a bit painful.

JJ's abdomen was getting bigger and with regular checkups the doctor said the baby was growing nicely. JJ looked absolutely ravishing. Her cheeks were pink and full, and she ate like a horse. She'd put on pounds, and she really looked quite lovely with the added weight.

He was an emotional wreck. Torn between wondering how their little baby would look to praying the kid was healthy to what in the world had he been thinking getting JJ pregnant?

To top it off, he was still nervous when he watched JJ take off in the float plane which she'd been doing every morning after breakfast. It was her "morning walk" she said. Flying made her feel free and she loved practicing her takeoffs and landing on the water. Every time she left his sight in that white plane, an inner nervousness took hold and it vanished the instant she came home an hour or so later.

This morning she hadn't gone out because she'd readied up the house. This afternoon their new helper, whom they had hired on a temporary basis through Cowboys Online, would be flying in with a pilot from North Country Air.

Jenna had called last week and confirmed that Milena Allen, JJ's old cell-mate qualified for a temporary two-week leave from the penitentiary. But she would have to return there once her work assignment here was complete. Once Jenna could find a permanent assignment for Milena then she would get parole just like JJ had.

Brady still wasn't sure he liked the idea of having an inexperienced woman look after the ranch while they were away, but JJ had insisted Milena was reliable. He just wished he could have as much confidence in this stranger as she did. The two women had been conversing through email and phone calls getting to know one another again. JJ had also brought her up to speed as to what was required while they were away building the cabin.

Dan and Rafe had been out all day haying and were expected back tonight for supper. The hired lady hadn't even come yet and he already couldn't wait to get away with JJ and the guys. Although they would be roughing it by living in a tent until the floor and roof were on the building, the trip was kind of a vacation away from the normal everyday running of things.

As he stood on the back steps of the mudroom Brady tensed when he heard the distinct drone of a far off airplane engine. At that moment, JJ came rushing out the back door and stepped carefully down the steps.

She was in her second trimester now and damned if she didn't have the slightest waddle when she walked. Maybe it was his imagination, but he didn't think so.

She'd been overly excited about Milena's arrival and now that the time had finally arrived, she looked harried yet beautiful. Her hands were knotted together and she was nodding as if telling herself everything was going to be okay.

"She's here. Oh, my goodness, she's finally here," JJ whispered as she looked toward the south end of the lake where the sound of the plane came from.

Brady followed her gaze and sure enough, a float plane was flying in low over the treetops across the lake. As the plane angled down toward the lake, he noted the blue color and knew it was Blue who was bringing in Milena.

"I can't believe she is actually here," JJ gasped as she stared.

Brady expected that they'd start down to the dock to meet the plane but as he stepped forward, she just stood there, shaking her head. Her eyes were wide and frantic and she held her sweetly rounded belly with her hands, as if she were trying to comfort their baby. She looked like she might be having another anxiety attack. Or was something wrong with the baby?

Panic rushed through him. "What's the matter?"

"I don't know what to say to her? I haven't seen her in so long. She was such a life saver for me that one year we knew each other. I just don't know what to say."

Brady relaxed. That's all? Man, he needed to chill. This expectant father business was really stressful.

He held out his hand to her and smiled. She was so cute when she was flustered.

"You can start by saying hi, how are you doing? Glad you came."

JJ nodded jerkily, reached out and grabbed his hand. He squeezed her fingers with reassurance.

"Yeah, okay. I can do that. I can do that."

I can't do this. What in the world was I thinking getting Melina to come all the way here to the middle of nowhere? What if she doesn't like it here? What if she is afraid of being alone? Why hadn't I asked her all these questions before making her come here?

JJ felt as if her head was going to bust with all these questions as Brady pulled her along the trail. He commented on how the day had turned out pretty nice considering the nasty thunderstorm they'd had again last night. But she really hadn't noticed the storm. It had been Dan's turn to spend the night with her and she'd lain snug and cozy in his strong arms, feeling so safe, while the lightning had flickered wildly at his bedroom windows and the thunder had made the bed tremble.

White steam uncurled through the air as the sunshine hit the dirt path. Silver sparkles glinted off the white-capped waves and JJ swore if she wasn't so nervous she would have loved the picturesque view of the big blue float plane delicately landing on the lake. Any other time she would be happy to see Blue and ask questions about Blue's twenty-month-old baby girl, but today was very different. She was a nervous wreck.

She had quite a bit riding on Milena. The guys had put their faith in JJ and her recommendation of Milena being reliable. What if something went wrong? What if prison had changed her since they'd been together? What if she accidentally burned down the ranch? What if she decided to walk out of here and escape?

Stop the negative shit, JJ! You've chatted with her every day for weeks on the phone!

JJ's heart picked up speed as she spied the familiar tall woman stepping off the pontoon of the float plane that had just docked. It had been years since she'd seen her. Too many years.

When Milena raised her head and spied JJ, she held open her arms.

"Jennifer Jane!" Milena shouted out to her.

Oh, my goodness! She'd forgotten how sweet Milena's voice sounded. Like music. Happy music. And suddenly it was as if they had never been apart.

JJ wasted no time running down the length of the dock and into her old friend's embrace.

Unexpected tears and emotions welled up as Milena wrapped her arms around JJ and hugged her so tight that she could barely breathe. But it was a wonderful hug that dissolved all doubts.

Milena was perfect for this job.

After a long, peaceful minute, JJ pulled away. Neither said a word as they stared at each other.

Milena hadn't changed much. Her hair was still a plain brown, straight and shoulder length with bangs. There were tiny wrinkles at the sides of her smiling mouth where there hadn't been any before. Miniature wrinkles etched the edges of her dark brown eyes, but those eyes still twinkled with a genuine friendliness that had always drawn JJ toward the woman.

"My Lord, you look so beautiful. Pioneer life agrees with you," Milena whispered.

"I love it here, beats bars."

They both laughed and Milena's gaze drew to JJ's baby bump.

"Wow, so now you are going to have a baby," Milena said.

"Almost there."

"Hey, ladies. Make way for Milena's luggage," Blue called out as she appeared at the door of the plane with one small suitcase.

"Hi Blue. I'll take it," JJ reached out but Milena pushed her arm aside, stepping forward to take the suitcase.

"No, you can't, Jennifer Jane. You're pregnant."

"I'm pregnant, not an invalid. Gosh, you sound just like the guys," JJ huffed.

Milena smiled warmly and Blue laughed.

"I want to meet these guys, but first, give me another hug. You seem stressed."

JJ shook her head as Milena embraced her again. Wow, she'd forgotten how easily Milena had always been able to read her and calm her down.

"Sorry I can't stay, ladies. I've got another delivery to make. Have a nice visit. See you in a couple of weeks," Blue interjected from behind them.

"Thank you so much for bringing Milena out here. I really appreciate it," JJ said. "Give your baby a hug from me, will you?"

"And from me too!" Milena added.

"Will do." Blue smiled, waved and then slammed the door shut. Several moments later, the plane's pontoons were slapping against the rough water as Blue's plane streaked across the lake. Seconds later, the plane was airborne, then drifted over the treeline and then everything went silent again.

"Wow, I cannot believe I'm really here. I've seen places like this on the Net and never thought I would ever get to see it live. And the air smells so fresh," Milena whispered.

JJ nodded. She still remembered when she had first shown up here on the ranch. The lake had been frozen back then. Everything had been covered in snow, but the air had been as crisp and clean just as it was now.

"And you freaking fly a plane too. It looks really nice, JJ. I am so proud of you for all your accomplishments."

Milena gave JJ another hug.

"The first hug I gave you was the goodbye hug I got ripped off when they took me out of there without even saying goodbye to you. Man, I am so sorry about that. I cannot give you enough apology hugs. But this bear hug is the oh my gosh I am so happy to see you hug."

JJ laughed as Milena squeezed JJ tighter and pure happiness melted through her.

When Milena let her go, JJ was once again able to breathe.

"I am so glad you are here. I hope you are hungry because I have a feast whipped up for you. So, tell me. I want to hear everything that you've been up to."

Milena frowned and shrugged. "Not much. I am still officially a prisoner. Just on loan to you here. But I want to thank you for giving me this awesome vacation. And over dinner I can tell you about all those courses I have been taking over the years."

"Great. Come on, I want you to meet the baby's father, Brady."

"That him?" Milena nodded toward Brady who stood at the end of the dock waiting for them.

"That's him," JJ replied as she gazed at her man.

He was so handsome wearing a black T-shirt and his jeans. JJ loved the way the sunlight played with the golden highlights in his brown wavy hair.

"Very nice-looking man. You two make a cute couple."

"I only go after the best," JJ teased.

"Is he good to you, JJ?" Milena asked softly.

"He is. He makes me feel so safe and loved. I never knew something like this could even exist."

Milena chuckled and then intertwined her arm with JJ's and tugged her along to where they stopped in front of Brady.

JJ made the introductions and loved the way the two smiled at each other. She knew instinctively they would get along.

"I can take your suitcase up to the house," Brady offered. But once again Milena declined.

So, Brady led the way along the path toward the ranch house. As they walked, Milena gasped at a nearby woodpecker that cracked its beak noisily against a twisted pine tree. Then she giggled as she focused her attention to a chipmunk that scampered across the trail right in front of them.

Wow, it felt as if years hadn't separated them and all the emotions of remembering her time in prison came rushing back. Milena had always been so upbeat and naturally curious about everything. She had been able to draw JJ out of her shell and her cell during the time they'd been together.

Despite not wanting to remember that time, the memories poured through her. Of not wanting to leave the safety of her cell to go and eat. Not wanting to take any courses. Just not wanting anyone to bother her or associate with the other cons. But Milena had prodded and nudged and made friends with JJ, coaxing her out of her shell.

JJ swallowed back the emotions and as they neared the ranch house Brady made the excuse he had to do some work in the barn and left them alone. She ushered Milena into the house and realized the woman hadn't stopped talking. She'd forgotten how talkative Milena could be too.

"This is such a beautiful place, JJ," she complimented as they entered the open concept kitchen, dining area and living room.

"Home sweet home," JJ said as she started the coffee machine.

"This place was made for you. The decor is quiet and natural, just like you," Milena said as she wandered into the living room and looked out the large back window.

JJ smiled at Milena's compliment.

"And you have a vegetable garden. How cool is that? No wonder you look so healthy. In prison, we die for fresh fruits and vegetables. Everything is canned or from frozen and—" She stopped, twirled around and clasped her hands to her chest.

"Sorry, you already know all the crap food we get. You were there. Hey, whatever you are cooking it smells really really good. I swear I am drooling."

"We're having roast beef. From one of our own cattle. Vegetables from the garden and mashed potatoes."

Milena closed her eyes and inhaled deeply.

"Smells like I died and went to heaven."

JJ nodded. She still felt that way every day.

"Is the lady here?" Rafe asked as he stepped out of the shed where he and Dan had just parked their tractors. Dan followed behind him and they circled Brady awaiting details.

They'd been excited all day long, wondering about the woman JJ had been talking almost non-stop about since Jenna had called with the news that Milena was allowed to come here for a temporary stay. But they'd been so busy with work and JJ had always been around during mealtimes, he hadn't been able to get much of a background scoop on this newcomer.

"She came in about half an hour ago. She seems nice," Brady answered with a shrug. He didn't make a move toward the ranch house.

"So? How come you're out here? Are you scared the newbie will bite?" Dan chuckled. Rafe rolled his eyes. Dan and his sense of humor.

"Thought it best to give them some alone time. After we eat, we take care of the dishes so JJ and Milena can spend more time getting reacquainted," Brady ordered.

His voice was laced with a crustiness Rafe had noticed was happening more and more often since the tetanus episode.

He wasn't overly concerned about Brady's attitude. Being in a similar situation just last year, he understood how frustrating it was to be cooped up and how humbling it felt to face death head on. The thought he might never see JJ again had probably shocked the shit out of Brady, just as it had Rafe.

"She seems very nice. I can see why JJ likes her," Brady replied.

"So, what was she in for again? I hadn't wanted to ask in front of JJ and this is about the only time we got you alone," Dan said.

Brady frowned and took on a serious tone.

"The sheet that Jenna faxed over said Milena is doing a maximum sentence. She's been inside for about thirteen years. Has had good behaviour and proven she can be reliable with many jobs in the prison. She's doing twenty years for murdering a security guard while robbing a jewelry store.

She wasn't the one who pulled the trigger, but she was with the guy who did. They were both high on drugs at the time. There were a couple other people involved in the confrontation but apparently their families had hired top-notch lawyers and were able to get them lesser sentences for testifying against Milena and her boyfriend."

"That's rough. Sorry I asked," Dan said.

"But she's off the drugs, right?" Rafe asked. He was concerned about the drugs. The last thing he wanted was for JJ to be around a woman who dabbled in narcotics.

"She seemed to be fine. Very friendly. They did random drug tests on her since she got accepted into the programs and she's been clean every time," Brady answered.

"Well, that's good to know," Dan said.

Rafe grunted affirmation.

He would be keeping an eye on her before they left to build that cabin. If he suspected in the slightest that she was using, he'd call Jenna and tell her to get the woman's ass back to prison.

Dan clapped his hands and the noise grabbed Rafe's attention.

"Well, I don't know about you two, but I am starving. Let's get our asses in there, meet this woman and eat!"

"If I remember right, Milena, you play a mean game of poker," JJ complimented as she poured coffee into the mugs and set them onto a platter with the homemade raspberry cheesecake, she'd made last night for this occasion.

"I gave up playing cards years ago," Milena answered.

Rafe, Dan and Brady were settled in the living room after JJ had ushered them out so she and Milena could get desert ready for everybody.

Instincts told her that Brady and Dan were happy with Milena but she noticed a bit of a wariness from Rafe. He'd been a quieter than usual but thankfully Rafe was covering up beautifully with good manners. But JJ made a note to ask him when they were alone what was bothering him.

She'd been proud of the compliments everyone had heaped onto her with the roast beef dinner she'd made. Milena had helped herself to three servings and no matter how much JJ coaxed her into helping herself to another serving, Milena had claimed a full stomach.

But as JJ put Milena in charge of carving up large slices of cheesecake for the guys and themselves, Milena's eyes sparkled with appreciation while she gazed at the pretty swirls of cream cheese icing.

"Oh my gosh, girlfriend. You are going to kill me with all this absolutely delicious eye festival food," Milena said with a laugh.

"We can work it off later with a walk," JJ said.

"I would absolutely love that. Hmm, I guess I can allow myself a slice of cake then?" Milena asked.

JJ nodded.

"Of course you can. Two or three slices if you want."

"Hey, as long as you leave lots for me," Brady called out as the guys started playing their traditional after dinner card game.

"Milena, you're more than welcome to join us in playing cards," Dan said from his favorite perch on one end of the sofa.

"Thanks, but I'll keep JJ company. We have so much to catch up on," Milena said with a smile. Then she turned to JJ. "You don't mind, do you?"

"Of course not," JJ answered. She was thrilled now that Milena was here. Having another woman to talk to was a treat.

"After you guys have your cake, we're doing the dishes so you can go for that walk," Rafe said as he suddenly appeared beside Milena. She handed him two plates, and then she followed him into the living room with another plate which she handed to Brady.

"Wow, Milena you'll have to stay forever, then I won't ever have to do the dishes again," JJ teased.

The men laughed at JJ's comment and then they dug into their desert while Milena poured everyone coffee.

JJ smiled as she watched her old friend. She seemed to enjoy the guys' company. She teased them with jokes about how she thought the ranch house was made just for JJ.

Over dessert the five of them discussed the cabin that was going to be built and then JJ and Milena made their excuses to go for that walk, both reminding the men of their promise to do the dishes.

"It's absolutely heaven here, JJ," Milena said from behind JJ as they strolled along an overgrown animal path that meandered near the shoreline of the lake.

JJ had walked along here sometimes, but never this far on her own.

"There are a bunch of blueberries about an hour up this trail. They usually ripen around the end of July. But no one has any time to go and pick them." JJ said as she continued walking. They had already been on the trail half an hour and she knew they should be starting back now.

But the air smelled so fresh and clean and it was so quiet out here.

"And I don't want you going off by yourself when you are here alone, either," JJ warned. "I want you to promise me you'll stick close to the ranch house or walk the all-terrain vehicle paths only just like we've discussed."

When she didn't hear a response from Milena, JJ stopped and turned around. Milena was standing about twenty feet away looking out over the picturesque lake. She had such a peaceful expression on her face that JJ remained quiet so Milena could take in the beauty of the glass-like blue lake water, the quietness of the scenery and the loon that was watching them from nearby.

"What's that?" Milena suddenly asked as she pointed out across the water to the v-shaped line with a small dot in front of the V. The black dot was heading away from them at a brisk speed.

"A beaver," JJ answered. "We have several of them down at the end of this trail. There's a big beaver dam with a small waterfall near those blueberries I was telling you about."

"Can we go look?"

JJ shook her head as she gazed at the dropping sun.

"We need to head back. It's getting late. The last thing we want to be doing is to travel the trail at night, who knows what we'll encounter out here."

Uneasiness made JJ brush past Milena.

"Oh, spooky. That's right up my alley," Milena laughed as she followed JJ.

As they headed back, they reminisced about some of the prison women they'd had the pleasure of knowing while incarcerated. By the time they reached the ranch, twilight was making it difficult to see the last few minutes on the trail, but the porch light was shining like a welcome beacon. She heard the door creak open and the men were quickly stepping out and sauntering down the steps.

Relief splashed on all their faces as Milena and JJ walked up the path to meet them.

"We were just about ready to send out a search party, baby mamma," Brady said. He stepped forward and gave JJ a quick kiss. She longed for a deeper, more intimate kiss, but with Milena watching, she didn't want to make her uncomfortable, so JJ resisted the overwhelming urge to reaching out and grab Brady and planting one full on his lips. And if Milena hadn't been here, she'd be planting big kisses on Rafe and Dan as well.

"Sorry, we got lost in conversation," Milena announced. "Won't happen again. Cross my heart and hope to die."

Brady chuckled.

"The dishes are done. We're going to head into the barn. Milena, would you like us to show you around?"

Milena nodded eagerly.

"You all go ahead. Rafe, can I talk to you for a minute?" JJ said quickly.

"Oh, oh, Rafe's in trouble," Milena commented and punched him in the arm. Rafe said nothing, but thankfully chuckled.

When they were all out of earshot, JJ frowned.

"What's wrong?" she asked him.

Rafe averted her gaze and gazed down toward the lake. When he didn't say anything, JJ continued.

"I was picking up just a bit of tension where Milena is concerned. Is there something you don't like about her?" she asked quietly.

"She seems nice. I was just concerned about her history with drugs."

JJ frowned. She had no idea where he was going with this. She already knew about Milena's drug problem past. She also knew from Jenna that the prison had done random drug tests on Milena.

"I don't understand."

He inhaled slowly and then exhaled a sigh.

"Our house was always full of foster kids. My mom and dad loved them all, but some of them were into drugs and there was a pattern I noticed about those specific kids."

"What kind of pattern?"

"The old saying misery loves company is true."

"What are you talking about, Rafe?" Being confused irritated her these days, thanks to those ever-loving hormones.

"Drug users tend to drag others into their world. I don't want that happening to you."

Shock reverberated through her. How could Rafe say something like that to her? She refrained from exploding on him. He needed to say his peace and she needed to stay calm.

"And I'm just not a hundred percent comfortable leaving her here alone on the ranch. She was a drug user and users tend not to be reliable. Had I known her past I might not have agreed to this."

JJ's irritation turned to anger.

"She's not using, Rafe. It's history. Give her a break, please?"

Rafe's eyebrows furrowed. She could tell he wasn't listening to her.

"Give her a chance, Rafe. What she did was twelve or thirteen or more years ago. The tests proved she is clean. We wouldn't have allowed her to come here and take care of the ranch if we had any doubts that she couldn't handle it. At least I wouldn't have brought her here if I had any doubts. And do you seriously think that I could be so easily swayed into the world of drugs? Don't you trust me?"

Rafe swore softly. To her amusement, his face blushed red with embarrassment.

Good! It served him right for realizing he was wrong. However, she understood his concern.

He reached out and curled his hands over her shoulders. He squeezed gently. His eyes sparkled with sudden enjoyment.

"Of course, I do. Man, you sure know how to make a man feel guilty."

"I'm sorry I snapped at you," JJ soothed. "I just want you to be happy and to be at ease while we are away. Can you at least try to relax? You're too uptight. I doubt anyone else noticed there was some tension during dinner. But I noticed."

Rafe grinned and growled.

"I know one way to relax," he whispered.

JJ giggled as she caught his meaning.

"Any other time, you would have me sneaking away with you," she admitted.

Rafe nodded. "Yeah, me too. This next couple of weeks is going to be a bitch without you in my bed."

Instincts told her that he might lower his head to kiss her and she wanted to feel his hot mouth upon her lips. But she didn't want Milena to see anything and ask questions. It was her private business having three men all to herself.

When Rafe began to lower his head, just like she suspected, she reached up and slapped her hands upon his hot chest, stopping him cold.

A low grumble of frustration erupted in Rafe's throat and rumbled through JJ as well. It would be so nice to run back into the ranch house and have Rafe make love to her upstairs in bed. Despite having company, her cravings for sex were still alive and well.

She almost caved into the idea of telling him to run upstairs for a quickie. Almost.

Thankfully, Rafe moved away from her. He grabbed her hand and tugged her toward the barn.

"Come on, we'd better go and help Brady and Dan show Milena around. The more she knows about this place, the better I will feel about leaving her here alone."

JJ smiled. She'd won Rafe over to Milena's side. Suddenly she had the feeling everything was going to be all right now.

Chapter Eight

MILENA PLACED HER HANDS on her hips and stared with pride at the two full buckets of blueberries that she'd placed in the shade of one of the blueberry bushes.

Wow! Could she pick blueberries? Or could she pick blueberries? She'd been a mean, lean, blueberry picking machine and had the buckets filled within an hour. The bushes had been robust with blue. There were still so many berries begging to be picked, it was a shame to leave them behind. She wished she had a tent. She would pitch it right there, camp out with a nice little fire and eat berries for suppers.

However, she only had two hands and very full heavy buckets and it was getting late afternoon. She needed to start heading back to the ranch.

She turned her attention to the shimmering lake in front of her. The tips of the waves glittered like white diamonds and the silhouette of pine trees far off on the other side of the lake made her wish she had the cheap watercolor paint set she'd left back at the prison. She ached to dab the scenery onto some paper and bring the painting back to the prison to hang up in her cell.

She shuddered at the thought of going back to lockup and immediately put the thought out of her mind. She wasn't going to waste a second of her freedom thinking about the inevitable.

Instead, she would have to commit the scenery to memory. She watched as a couple of big dark-colored birds skimmed low over the water and finally landed in the waves. The birds began singing a mournful sound that sent shivers up her spine.

Loons. She'd heard them cry every day and every night. They were lucky that they could fly like JJ and now swim so leisurely in the water, apparently with no worries in the world.

A nice leisurely swim would cool her down too. She was ultra-warm having walked along the shore in the sunshine to get here and then another hour picking in the heat. Unfortunately, she'd always been afraid of water. She had no idea why, but ever since she could remember, she hadn't been a fan.

No baths for her. Showers were the exception. Swimming was so not happening in her lifetime. She wiped the sweat from her forehead and inhaled the fresh, crisp mid-August air.

Despite her boredom, this place certainly was as close to a heaven she could imagine. It was quiet, joyful and peaceful.

Even though JJ had mentioned to Milena that she shouldn't stray far from the ranch house while she was alone, she'd been going bat-shit stir crazy with boredom by the time her chores were finished every morning.

She'd loved doing the chores; taking care of the garden. Making sure that the few older cattle the guys had in the barn where well fed and their stalls clean. Chores were not the problem. She did everything that needed doing for the past almost two weeks since they'd been gone. She'd even forced herself to follow a few recipes in one of JJ's cookbooks. But cooking never had interested her, so her creations were crap compared to JJ's delicious food.

Milena did look forward to her only human contact by phone when JJ or one of the fellows or even when the parole officer called in daily to see how she was coming along.

Truth be told, she'd been lonely here. In prison, there was always someone around yapping or being a pest and back there she'd craved peace and quiet every day and night. Now that she had it, it was driving her nuts.

Milena licked her dry lips, suddenly realizing she was pretty thirsty. She hadn't brought along any water. Hadn't even thought of it.

She sighed as she eyed the lake. During one of their endless conversations over the past weeks, she remembered JJ had mentioned that they got their ranch water out of a drilled well, but that the lake water was also clean and free of pollutants and drinkable.

That's what she would do. She could cup her hands and use them to quench her thirst. Yet, she wasn't sure she wanted to get *that* close to the water.

Oh, come on, silly girl. Be brave!

Milena took a deep breath and forced her legs to move. Gingerly, she stepped around some sharp rocks and tried not to stumble over the abundance of bushes that laced the shoreline. By the time she'd reached about one foot from the lake, her heart was pounding and she had horrible visions of a giant arm of water curling out, grabbing her, and pulling her right into the lake, drowning her.

Shit, talk about your crazy imagination going wild.

But she was thirsty and desperate times did call for desperate measures. She stepped as close to the shore as she dared, squatted as best she could, and was glad to see the water wasn't bottomless at all. She could see rippled sand there at the bottom. She guessed the water was only a foot deep.

She sighed with relief.

Freaking out over nothing, silly.

She let out a laugh, leaned over, cupped her hands, and dipped them into the liquid. She sighed at the wonderful coolness that washed over her fingers. The water was clear.

Quickly, she lifted her cupped hands and gingerly sipped.

Tastes good.

She took more sips and then gulps as she kept dunking her hands into the lake. The water surely hit the spot and when she drank her fill, she stood, turned, and froze.

Oh my God!

Some big black, furry creature, twice as big as her, was casually strolling on four big legs toward her two buckets of blueberries!

"Hey! Get! Get out of here!" Milena shouted. The instant she yelled, she realized maybe she shouldn't have drawn attention to herself?

The bear stopped. Its short, rounded ears twitched and then it turned its furry black head and gazed at her with what appeared to be curiosity. It had a short black snout and a black nose that twitched as it smelled the air.

Wasn't there something about bears that she'd read once? Not to get between mother and baby bears?

As the bear stood still and stared at her, she surveyed the nearby surroundings. No sign of any little ones. A sliver of relief whispered through her.

"Hi," she said to the bear.

The bear sniffed the air some more. Huh, he or she seemed to be harmless enough.

"Listen, get away from my buckets, and then I will be on my merry way." She spoke to the big creature like she would to a human.

Like the damned thing understands me?

She suddenly remembered something else she'd read. Make noise. Lots of noise so the bear would know you were in the area. Was that before or after encountering a bear?

Oh crap, she couldn't remember.

JJ had mentioned that they rarely had a bear around the ranch house, mainly because bears didn't like humans and she tended to sing or smack sticks against trees while out for a walk to keep it noisy.

But this bear seemed to like people. It wasn't leaving. Nor was it moving away from her buckets. Actually, the bear was ignoring her and was following his sniffing nose now toward her blueberry-filled buckets!

"Hey! Wait a minute! Get away from my buckets! Oh, come on! Stop already!" Milena shouted as high as she could. She ran toward the bear and stopped about fifteen feet away.

From here she got a closeup view of paws and claws. She remembered seeing a movie once of some pioneer guy wearing a necklace made from bear claws. Maybe she shouldn't be getting so close?

However, the bear continued to zero in on those buckets like it was a heat-seeking missile.

Milena huffed with frustration.

"Oh, come on! Please!" she yelled.

It continued toward the buckets.

Anger burned through her. *Son of a bitch!*

Gazing around the ground in front of her, she spied a couple of soft-ball sized rocks. Maybe she could scare it away by throwing them near it?

She grabbed the rocks and quickly tossed one. It plopped onto the ground a couple of feet in front of the bear.

It stopped, turned and looked at her again. This time it growled. It was an ominous sound that sent shivers up her spine. She spied some mean-looking fang-like very long teeth too.

Time to back off. Bear did not look happy.

"Okay, okay, maybe I should just leave?"

Forget the blueberry buckets. Get out of here!

She could always come back another time with JJ and pick some. Suddenly she got a really bad feeling that she had made a very big mistake in coming here alone. She should have listened to JJ more carefully when she'd been told not to venture away from the ranch house. She should have obeyed JJ when she'd said not to come along this trail that first evening she'd arrived here.

The bear kept growling at her and that's when she realized the creature was blocking the trail and her way back home.

She inhaled at the word home. Oh man, she really wanted to be back at the ranch house. She really enjoyed the chores. Loved the quietness. Just not the solitude. Was there a difference? She wasn't sure.

What should she do? What if after it ate her blueberries, it came after her? Where could she go? Into the water?

No.

She didn't like the way the bear kept studying her and growling and now it was even snorting. His eyes were black and evil-looking. Shivers ripped through her.

Maybe she should run? No, she wasn't supposed to do that. She'd read not to run. Or was it the other way around?

She *really* wanted to run.

The bear turned toward her. Sniffed the air some more. Growled again. Took a step forward. It licked its lips with a long tongue.

Oh damn. Was she tonight's dinner?

"If you move, she will attack you. Just stay still. I will take care of her, just don't move," a man said. His voice was calm and came from somewhere off to her left about twenty feet away right by the lakeshore.

Milena didn't move. Dared not look to see who was talking. Dared not even take a risk to answer him. Heck, she wasn't even going to nod to acknowledge that she had heard him.

Fear rocked her. It was like the horrific sinking feeling of dread that she'd experienced after she'd seen all that blood blossom across that security guard's chest when her boyfriend had shot him all those years ago. It was a bad feeling. Really bad.

Instincts told her the bear was going to attack her, just like this guy said.

Great, she'd get killed by a bear on her first outing from prison. Wait until the mates back at the prison heard about this one. They'd laugh and joke with each other that she just could not catch any luck.

Defiance rocked through her. If need be, she would poke the bear in the eyes. Blind it, and run!

Milena jerked at the harsh sound of the man as he suddenly yelled the words. "Get the hell out of here!"

His shouts were quickly followed by some clanging sound like metal on metal that really hurt her ears.

The bear whipped its head toward the noise.

Milena forced herself to remain as still as a statue despite wanting to run for her life.

"Get! Move on! Get!" The man shouted. The clanging grew louder and quicker. She swore that noise would drive her nuts if it kept up.

The bear grunted loud, turned away from Milena and suddenly sauntered through the blueberry bushes and disappeared.

"Okay, she's gone. You can relax."

Milena found herself nodding like she was some bobblehead. The man suddenly appeared in front of her.

My, he was big. Yep, big guy. He didn't scare her. Well, not as much as the bear did.

She stared up at him. Noticed he was a head taller than her and kind of handsome in a rugged, outdoorsy sort of way. His hair was short, military short. Light brown with gold highlights. Eyes were friendly and chocolate brown.

"Are you okay, ma'am?" he asked. Concern etched in his face.

"Um, I think so," she croaked. She was shaking like a leaf.

He had big shoulders. He wore a plain V neck short-sleeved dark green shirt that matched the forest behind him. Military dog tags dangled from a silver chain necklace from his neck.

A soldier? Out here in the wilderness? Weird.

"There is a chance the bear might come back. Are you alone here, ma'am?"

Why did that question sound so ominous?

Nope, she was not answering that question.

He held up two dented stainless-steel pots with blackened bottoms.

"You did the right thing in screaming. Bears don't like noise. But it sensed your fear. Next time just make sure you bring a bell or whistle or something like these pots and use it every few minutes so the bears will know you're here. They'll stay away."

Milena's gut clenched.

"Bears? Like in more than one? How many?"

He looked at her as if to say, "Are you serious?".

"The wilderness is full of them. Full of man-eating beavers and head-stomping moose too. You just have to make some noise."

Was he kidding her?

Man-eating beavers? Head-stomping moose? Why hadn't JJ warned her that this place was so dangerous?

"You must be the lady who is taking care of Moose Ranch?" He suddenly placed the two pots onto the ground, stepped forward and extended his hand.

She nodded shakily and extended her hand. It shook wildly.

"Yes. Yes. I am."

"I'm Daegen. And you are?"

"Milena."

"Pleasure to meet you, Milena."

His grip was strong and warm and for the briefest moment she felt safe. When he let go, she was thrust back into her world of aloneness.

"Where did you come from?" she asked. JJ had said there was no one around for miles.

"Was fishing just at the mouth of the river about five minutes off. Best trout ever. Had a big one on the line, but your screaming distracted me to the point the fish yanked the fishing pole into the lake with it. I had two choices. Dive into the lake and chase after the fishing rod and let you get mauled by the bear. Or come and rescue you."

Guilt rammed into her. "I am so sorry. I owe you a fishing rod."

He shook his head.

"Don't worry about it. It's just a handmade cedar pole with some fishing line and a hook. Quite primitive."

Primitive like him. Now that her fear was settling down a little, she noticed the bristly five o'clock shadow hugging his chin and cheeks. He was dressed in jeans and he wore...moccasins? How interesting.

"Do you know your way back?" he asked.

She nodded. "Just follow the lakeshore animal trail and I'll run smack into the ranch house."

"That's right. The bear is probably long gone by now. So, you should be safe."

Probably gone? Should be safe?

Shit! Suddenly she wasn't sure she wanted to go back alone, especially with the man-eating beavers and head-stomping moose. But she couldn't ask him to escort her. She didn't even know him. Maybe he was a killer who was camped out here eluding the police?

Okay. Calm down. He is not a killer.

She tensed as he walked over to the two buckets overfilled with her blueberries.

He grunted. A low rumble of thunder followed his grunt.

Oh great. Another freaking storm.

"Those pails are gonna get heavy before long and it looks like rain. How about I give you a lift back in my canoe."

Yeah, so you can kill me?

Another low rumble of thunder. This time closer.

He looked to the sky and frowned. She followed his gaze and her tummy dipped in a bad way. Huge black clouds were rolling toward the sun.

"Actually, I will have to insist I give you a ride. The storm is coming in fast. It's not safe to be outdoors with the lightning we get around here. We need to head out now, before the waves get bad."

Without waiting for an answer, he picked up her buckets, turned and hurried along the shoreline in the direction he'd come from earlier.

Okay now was her chance to escape. He could have the blueberries. She turned to run but then stopped. The trees were swaying in the increasing wind and she could hear branches cracking.

Then lightning flickered.

Oh crap! She was not in the mood for getting hit by lightning and get all cooked up for the bears. She had no choice but to follow him. But how was she *ever* going to get up enough nerve to get into a canoe?

The last thing Daegan needed was a damned female on his hands. And a freaking greenhorn to boot, he thought as he placed the two heavy buckets of blueberries beneath the front seat of his bright red wood canoe and repositioned his cooler full of fish in front of the buckets.

"Okay, hop in while I hold the canoe steady," he said as he held tight to the edge of his boat.

She didn't move. She just stared at his canoe as if it was that bear he'd just chased off. Like she was paralyzed with terror.

"Ma'am, you really need to get a move on," he prodded.

Lightning slashed through the sky overhead. Thunder complained angrily.

Shit! Time to go, lady!

"I won't hurt you. I'm gay," he lied. Maybe that would calm her down?

"It's n-not that. I don't like water." She was shaking her head and he sensed she would run off.

He almost laughed aloud. She was afraid of water? Man, he just could not catch a break today. Lost his fishing rod, and now a chick who was giving him grief with a looming thunderstorm.

He grabbed the spare red life jacket from beneath the middle seat of the canoe.

"This is a life vest. If you wear it and fall into the water, nothing will happen to you as it will allow you to float."

"It will?" she blinked at him. Man, she was pretty. She had a smile in her eyes even when she was frightened. How cool was that?

"Watch how I put mine on and you do the same. Okay?"

She nodded and jumped as thunder cracked overhead.

"We'll be fine. You're wearing rubber soled running shoes. Lightning won't hit the boat as long as you keep those shoes on." He hoped that wasn't a lie, but the thought popped into his mind. Hopefully it would calm her a little.

He reached for his vest. She watched as he showed her how to put it on and followed suit. A moment later, she was all geared up.

"Good job. Now, next step..."

He grabbed her wrist and placed it on the edge of the canoe.

"Hold here. Stay hunched and just lift one foot across the rim and then the other. Try to stay in the middle of the boat. Sit down on the centre bench and hold onto the sides while I get in. Got it?"

"Uh, huh."

Concern gripped him. She looked pale as a ghost as she stared at the waves crashing against the side. She *really* was afraid of water.

He kept his hand over hers as she slowly moved a leg over and then the other. Man, she sure did have a nicely shaped butt. He blinked that thought away with a shake of his head.

Concentrate on the task at hand, my man.

He could tell she'd never been in a canoe before because she was all wobbly like a newborn colt. He held her hand until she plopped very unladylike onto the middle seat. He reminded her to hold onto the edges. He figured it would help stabilize the now rocking canoe as he climbed in.

As he sat on the seat behind her, the wind blew a lungful of her very pretty scent his way. She smelled of watermelon. Probably some shampoo or perfume that she used.

He was reacting to her smell, despite not wanting to. His cock was jerking against his jeans and waking up from one hell of a long sleep.

Right now, was not the time. The storm was coming in fast and there was some heavy duty paddling to do. He doubted she knew how to paddle, so he didn't bother to ask and there was no time to show her.

The sunshine disappeared and everything went gray. Drops of rain began to fall.

"Hold on! It's going to be a rough ride!" he yelled above the shrieking wind.

Hell, if they were lucky, they just might make it back to Moose Ranch. If they weren't...then he hoped she knew how to swim.

Chapter Nine

"MY GOODNESS, THIS IS absolutely fancy. Too fancy for out here in the middle of nowhere," JJ whispered as she stood in front of the newly built log cabin. She'd just returned from flying Paul and Mitch back to their ranch. She would have swung by to check in on Milena but because JJ wanted to spend a night alone with her guys, she'd bypassed the ranch and returned here to her cowboys.

Besides, tomorrow they would return to Moose Ranch and she could spend the remaining couple of days with Milena. In the meantime, she loved looking at this cabin.

It had been erected by her three men as well as Paul and Mitch. Paul, who had learned everything there was to know about masonry, compliments of his father, had with Brady's help, who slung a mean cement trowel, made the two stone fireplaces. One at each end of the building. The chimneys were exquisite and had been made from the stones and rocks found in abundance around the surrounding wilderness and meadows.

"Nothing is too fancy for Moose Ranch and her lady boss," Dan chuckled as he joined JJ. They both fell silent as they took in the sight.

The cabin was located near the water and the guys had nailed together a large, sturdy dock where the plane was now securely moored. They'd tied the plane with ropes to nearby sturdy trees to prevent it from bobbing to and fro due to the winds.

Being close to a lake, allowed JJ to fly them in at cattle roundup. They had purchased four new all terrain vehicles for the ranch and had flown the older vehicles out here. They were stored in a makeshift shed out back.

A hastily thrown together picnic shelter had housed the picnic table where she had served the guys their meals. The table had since been moved into the cabin kitchen and to her surprise the guys had strung up a hammock in the shelter so she could rest her curiously sore feet while cooking on the outdoor rock barbecue that Brady and Paul had also put together.

Behind the log cabin was also a rough atv trail. The path had been forged through a quarter mile of forest to hook up with the existing atv trail system which led to various pastures and meadows that housed their cattle. The railroad round-up area where the cattle would be corralled and shipped off to slaughter, was a mile away from here.

As the ranch grew, they had plans to hire a man or two to stay out here to keep an eye on the cattle. But that wasn't for another year or so.

"It all looks so perfect," JJ said as she hooked her arm with Dan and ushered him up onto the wood veranda. She smiled at the two rocking chairs at each end of the porch.

"These are new arrivals. Where did they come from?" she asked. She sat in one of the chairs and loved the gentle motion as she cradled her baby belly and rocked.

"Brady made them during his convalescence time out in the barn. Two more to be made," Rafe answered.

She leaned forward in her chair and spied Rafe. He stood just inside the screen door. Brady stood beside him, grinning like a Cheshire cat.

"Oh, Brady. They're beautiful. I love the rocking motion. It's very relaxing. I could stay here, forever" she complimented. She leaned back against the chair, closed her eyes, and inhaled the hot August air, and rocked.

"Well, you could do that. But supper is ready. We've got moose lasagna leftovers. Hot out of the pot," Dan stated.

At the mention of food, JJ's tummy growled and her mouth watered.

"Hand up?" Dan asked with a chuckle.

"Am I getting that big that I can't get out of a chair?" JJ laughed as she accepted his help. She was starting to feel a bit clumsy with her baby belly. How was she going to do another three plus months of this feeling this fat? And she hadn't even put on that many pounds.

You will. You can handle anything.

Somewhere to the south, thunder rumbled.

"Hmm, sounds like we're going to be having some good old-fashioned storm sex, tonight," JJ said softly as she followed the guys into the cabin.

All three of them tensed in front of her and stopped.

JJ laughed. "But first I need nourishment. Lots of nourishment, boys."

The men moved in unison. Dan held out a chair for her where they had placed it at the end of the picnic table in the kitchen area. Brady quickly doled out the moose lasagna and Rafe poured her some coffee. Such sweet men. Always looking to make her comfortable.

But tonight, she didn't want comfort. Tonight, she would demand her pleasure.

By the time they got to the dock, they were soaked and Milena was ready for a hot shower. She helped Daegen get the blueberry-filled buckets safely out of the boat and assisted him in dragging the canoe out of the water. Then to her surprise, he hoisted the canoe upside down and held it over their heads like an umbrella. He told her to grab the blueberries and to stay close to him.

When she had the buckets firmly in hand, they walked along the dock and then wandered up the trail that would lead to the ranch house.

Goodness, who knew someone could use a canoe as an umbrella?

The warm wind was ferocious and several times she almost fell on the slippery muddy trail. Wouldn't that be something? To have brought these berries all this way and to have them tip over into the mud.

She was shaking with a chill as Daegen ordered her up the outside stairs and into the house. Once she got inside, she placed the heavy pails onto the floor and watched through the mudroom window as he tipped the boat over.

Mercy, he had very nice muscled arms. She hadn't noticed out on the lake. She had been too busy praying for her life, hoping the canoe wouldn't tip over. If it had, she might have drowned in those two-feet high waves despite this constrictive device he'd put on her. She simply didn't know how to swim.

Thankfully her hero had kept the canoe from tipping.

"You can leave the vest right here on one of the hooks and then go grab yourself a shower before the power goes out and get on a change of clothes," he said as he unlatched his orange lifejacket, then slipped it up over his head. She quickly removed her jacket and placed it beside his on one of the free hooks just inside the door.

Despite it being warm in the mudroom, she was cold. Goosebumps popped out over her arms and she suddenly noted he was staring at her chest. Her gaze dropped to where he was looking. To her horror, her nipples poked against her very wet, suddenly too tight T-shirt.

Shit! She hadn't worn her bra today. Hadn't expected to run into anyone.

She turned away from him, suddenly feeling embarrassed. And very aware the two of them were strangers and alone together in a big house. A crazy idea suddenly popped through her mind. What would he say if he knew she hadn't had sex with a guy in over thirteen years?

Stop it, Milena! You are not the same girl you were when you were a teenager! She'd had a weakness for good-looking guys. Especially the one who had used her and gotten her sent to prison.

Nope, guys were off limits. Preferably for the rest of her life.

"I'm sure you can find some clothes in the room I'm using," she said. "There are some shirts and pants in the closet. Some boxers in a bottom drawer. The first door to your left. I'll grab some clothes from the room first and the shower is just across the hall. I'll use it first and then it'll be nice and toasty for your turn."

He merely grunted. She could feel his hot gaze as she slipped off her running shoes, and headed down to the room she'd just mentioned. JJ had told her the room she'd been using belonged to Brady and that JJ had placed some of her clothes in there for Milena to borrow, which she had because truth be told, the clothes the prison had supplied her with weren't that nice.

As she sifted through the closet, she found a pretty pink blouse. She then grabbed the extra pair of jeans she had brought along, and tiptoed to the door. She peeked out into the hallway expecting to see Daegen still standing in the mudroom, but there was no sign of him.

She rushed across the hall and slipped into the bathroom and quietly locked the door.

Safe and sound.

"Dishes are done," JJ announced as she handed Brady the last plate. He towel dried it and set it on a nearby stack, then picked them up and placed them into a pine cupboard that had been nailed together and screwed into the wall just this morning. There still weren't any doors on the cupboards but that would be a future project, along with caulking around the windows to keep out the bugs and draft, getting in a proper sink into the kitchen area instead of using pails for washing and for rinsing. They would also need a couple of plastic pipes that would be attached to the sink allowing the water to drain into a hole outside the cabin and away from the lake. The hole would have to be hand dug like a well and covered with a wood-planked lid to prevent animals or people from falling in.

There was no worry about the soap hurting the environment either, because they only used biodegradable soaps and detergents. Being environmentally friendly as much as possible was one of their priorities out here. Sometime in the future, they might even get a generator to pump water up out of the lake. But that wasn't a necessity. He and the guys were quite content lugging up pails of water from the lake when needed.

"Did I ever tell you how sexy you look wearing an apron?" Brady murmured as he set the dry cutlery into a Tupperware container and placed the lid, then quickly put the mugs up into the cupboard beside the plates.

He heard her gasp at his comment.

"Plenty of times" she whispered as she dried her hands on her apron.

"Turn around," he ordered.

Brady noticed the smile playing on her lips before she did as he asked. He sensed she knew where he was going with this conversation.

He quickly untied the apron.

"It's our last night here, baby mamma," he said as he folded and then placed the apron on the makeshift pine-planked countertop.

Lightning suddenly flashed at the dark windows. Thunder boomed nearby. But he barely heard the noise above the loud thumping of his heart.

He *needed* to be with JJ.

Being away from her for so many nights had been the purest torture imaginable. But they hadn't been able to be together because all the men had slept in one large tent and JJ had slept in a small one while they'd been building the cabin.

"Well, there would have been more nights if you had come to my tent," she suggested.

Brady grinned. They were doing a lot of that lately. Quietly thinking on the same subject at the same time. Just like an old couple in sync with each other.

Dan laughed from his perch at the kitchen table where he and Rafe were playing an after-dinner game of cards by the gas lantern light.

"What is so funny?" JJ asked as she put her hands onto her hips and glared at Dan. But Brady saw the amusement playing in her eyes.

"That's a one-man tent. No one could fit in there but you," Dan complained from behind the fanned cards he held in his hand in front of his face.

"It's a one-woman tent and I wasn't alone. I had the baby for company," she reminded him as she moved a protective hand over her swollen belly.

Brady loved it when she cradled the baby. Hell, she looked like a sexy she-mama bear when she did that.

"Besides, if we had gone to your tent, the other guys would have caught on. You're too noisy," Brady teased.

He stepped forward, curled a protective arm around her waist and then softly placed a forefinger over her mouth, stopping a protest he knew would come. Another flash of lightening blinked at the windows. She jumped as thunder crackled and the floorboards trembled beneath their feet.

Worry flashed in her eyes.

"Shh, you're safe with us, JJ. Always safe," Brady whispered so only the two of them heard.

"That's going to be one hell of a storm," Rafe muttered.

"There's one hell of a storm brewing in here too," Brady answered.

He wanted JJ beneath him and he suspected the guys wanted her just as bad.

And he wanted her *now*.

JJ trembled as both Rafe and Dan looked up at Brady's comment. She noticed all the men's eyelids had begun to droop with lust. She knew what that storm comment meant. They *wanted* her. And she wanted them too.

Brady brought her closer against his hot length and she gasped at the size of his erection as he pressed himself against her. The snap of cards being slapped onto the table and the scrape of chairs rippled through the air as Dan and Rafe scrambled to their feet. The two men flanked Brady who let go of her and stepped back.

Gosh, they all looked so handsome dressed in their tight T-shirts, work jeans and sexy five o'clock shadows. She watched with intense awareness as all three men began to unbuckle their belts.

"If I didn't know any better, I'd say I'm in some hot strip club," she said with a laugh.

The men cursed softly. They smiled at her playful comment. But said nothing.

Rain pounded the sheet metal roof, creating a really cool backdrop of music for the strip show.

JJ's breath quickened as they slowly, erotically slipped off their pants. Their erections pressed boldly against their underwear. She could make out the thick impressions of their swollen cocks and a pleasing hunger raged inside her. She licked her suddenly dry lips. Noticed how all three men focused on her mouth.

Suddenly they moved faster. Yummy muscles bulged in their arms as they lifted off their T-shirts.

"You guys would do well in a strip club," she continued to tease. "I'm sorry but I didn't bring any money to stuff into your G-strings."

"You're all we'll ever need, sweetness," Rafe replied.

He stepped forward and she noticed him nod to Brady and Dan, indicating that the two go to one of the three small bedrooms toward the back end of the cabin. JJ remembered that's where the four new single mattresses for the bunk beds had been placed this morning.

"You shouldn't tease us like this, baby," Rafe whispered as he looked down at her with his gorgeous brown eyes. She knew he was teasing her back.

His sexy dark look encouraged JJ to move closer to him. She lifted her hand and tenderly touched his stubbled cheek. A muscle flexed beneath her fingertips. His breath quickened.

"You know I would never send you to a strip club, I would keep you all to myself."

Rafe chuckled as he drew down his head and muttered softly against her mouth.

"You have your own personal he-haram. How good is that?"

"More than good, sexy man. I am the luckiest woman in the world." She dropped her hand from his face and placed her palms over his ultra warm chest muscles. His hands settled on her waist and he gently rubbed his belly against her baby bump. She always laughed when one of her men branded her with his belly. The guys didn't have any jealousy toward one another. They just acted so normal with each other.

"We need to get you out of these clothes, but first," he whispered.

She moaned as he pressed his lips against hers, the fiery pressure encouraging her to open her mouth. His tongue dipped between her lips and licked her teeth and gums. The impact sent shudders of anticipation through her.

He broke the kiss and his hands slipped beneath her shirt. She lifted her arms allowing him to remove her top. Because the other men had been around, she had worn her bra, but Rafe wasted no time unclasping and removing the garment.

Her breasts spilled free and JJ gasped as he palmed her sensitive mounds.

"They are getting so big," he whispered.

She trembled as he dipped his head and enveloped one of her plump nipples between his strong lips.

Due to her pregnancy, all her intimate parts were very responsive. This time was no exception. The pressure of his lips around her nipple and the sharp friction of his stubble against her flesh had her crying out from the pleasure pain.

"Sorry, baby," he muttered. He eased off a little.

"Never be sorry for what is natural," she whispered. She caught his nipples between her fingers and he groaned as she erotically twisted.

His suckling deepened and sparklers went off behind her closed eyes. She felt heady, in a really good way.

Suddenly, she sensed someone behind her.

"Our bed is ready in the other room, baby," Dan said in a thick voice. His fingers slipped beneath the waistband of her maternity pants and panties. She moaned softly as her garments were lowered over her hips, thighs, and then down her legs.

With Rafe still suckling at her breast and his hot hands cupping her, she managed to step out of her clothes. She swallowed as a slurp of lube followed. Hissed and closed her eyes as a finger pressed pressure against her sprinter.

"Just relax, sweetie," Dan suggested as he prodded.

She managed to loosen up and his finger slipped into her. He pushed lube against her muscles while softly massaging and exploring. Having two men touching her so intimately, sent her awareness into overdrive. She sensed Brady was somewhere in the room too now, watching what Dan and Rafe were doing to her.

She managed to get her eyes open and sure enough, she spied Brady standing a few feet to her left. He was completely naked and stroking his thick, stiff cock. He caught her gaze and the impact of his hot stare just about melted her knees.

Had Rafe not been cupping her breasts and Dan not impaling her with a finger, she might have dropped to the floor, she was suddenly so weak with arousal.

Dan slipped two fingers into her, spreading more lube. Rafe moved his mouth to her other breast. He sucked and lapped on her nipple as if it were a lollipop, making her arch and hiss at the pleasure-pain sensations.

"She's ready," Dan whispered in a strangled voice. Suddenly Rafe let go of her nipple.

Before JJ knew what was happening, she was swept up into Rafe's strong arms. His eyes glittered in the lantern light as he carried her through the kitchen into the nearby bedroom. The room was dimly lit with several candles that had been set in what appeared to be a handmade wood white-birch chandelier that hung from the ceiling in the middle of the room. Wind blasted against the windows and the tiny flames on the candles flickered.

"Who made that?" she asked. It looked so quaint, like something pioneers would use.

"I did," Dan replied as he and Brady joined them.

"It's beautiful. We won't have to worry about power failures," she said.

Dan chuckled and he nodded to the wide bed that had been arranged upon the floor.

"Used three of the four mattresses and stretched them across. Wide enough for all of us," he said.

Rafe set her down upon her feet and instructed Brady to lie down on the mattresses. He did, stretching out down the middle of the makeshift bed that had been covered with sheets, blankets and pillows. Then Brady held his hand out for JJ.

"Come here, sweetheart," Brady said and wiggled his fingers. She nodded, feeling the heat of excitement roar through her. She stepped onto the mattress, laced her fingers with Brady's and then lay on her back beside him.

"Close your eyes, baby. Close your eyes and just feel what we're going to do to you."

Oh my!

She closed her eyes and felt Brady's hand slide over her breast. He tweaked the nipple Rafe had just been sucking on. Her flesh was sore, but pleasantly so, as he gently pinched and rubbed.

She blew out tense breaths while she listened to the rustling of clothing. Dan and Rafe were removing their underwear. Then she felt the mattress move and heard someone breathing on her other side.

"It's me, baby," Rafe said softly. She barely heard him above the sound of rain as it pounded upon the roof.

"This is kind of wild," JJ suddenly giggled. She couldn't help but to find this amusing.

There was a violent storm raging outside and she had three cowboys about to make love to her. How cool was that?

She heard Brady mumble something, but she couldn't make out what he'd said.

For a brief instant, she worried about Milena being back at the ranch, maybe a bit scared from all this thunder, but her worries disintegrated as Brady stopped playing with her nipple and then his hot, moist mouth replaced his fingers.

Rafe's lips curled around her other nipple. Both men began a gentle, erotic sucking while their hands tenderly slid over her belly bump, her inner thighs, and her breasts, igniting flames of pleasure everywhere they touched. Two tongues gently laved her nipples and then two sets of sharp teeth erotically nipped her tender flesh. Sharp, hot sensations rippled through her making her gasp.

"Lift your bum, sweetie," Dan instructed. She did as he asked and a pillow was quickly shoved beneath her butt.

Then her legs were being spread apart. The mattress dipped between her legs and she cried out and clenched her hands as Dan's hot mouth melted over her pussy. She bucked as his tongue laved her sensitized clit. His hands settled upon her hips and in her minds eye she could easily picture Dan's head dip between her thighs, his lips sucking her juices.

Her vagina muscles clenched in wicked want for penetration. She could feel the hot stickiness of her arousal easing along her channel.

Her orgasm mounted. It swelled through her. She began to tremble. To keen.

"She needs us," she heard Rafe groan.

Suddenly their hot mouths were gone from her breasts and her pussy. Someone was grabbing her by her waist, rolling her sideways and then she was being lifted into the air.

A moment later, she was gently lowered, her pussy stretched wonderfully as a shaft entered her. She struggled to open her eyes and when she finally did, she realized she'd been impaled upon Brady. His eyes were closed, and his face was etched with pleasure.

She slapped her hands upon Brady's chest, and began gyrating her hips, loving the sense of fullness deep inside of her.

Someone moved up against her backside and she instinctively leaned forward. As something hot and smooth nudged against her ass, JJ found Brady's mouth and kissed him.

He groaned and his shaft jerked inside of her. His tongue slipped into her mouth. Their tongues tangled and her senses blew apart.

A cock entered her ass in one swift thrust and JJ came apart. She shattered and convulsed as the climax rocked into her, sweeping her up in its tumultuous waves.

Thunder shook the cabin. Rain pummelled the windows and the men's groans intermingled with her cries. Wave after wave, pleasure made love to her.

The storm was relentless outside and inside.

JJ drifted in the sea of whispers, instructions and desire as lightning bolts of pleasure zipped through her. She convulsed and orgasmed beneath each man as they took turns with her. Eventually, when they were all satisfied, they fell asleep, fully spent and tangled together in an arrangement of arms, legs, sheets and blankets.

DAEGEN FROWNED AS THE lights flickered and a crack of thunder shook the floorboards beneath his feet. Another bad storm. They'd been having a run of storms lately with the days being so hot and humid.

The last thing he'd expected was for this day to end with a woman in it. He'd come out here to the seclusion of Northern Ontario for a reason. To get away from people and reality.

So much for trying to find peace. Instead, he'd found a cute woman.

He sighed and dumped the blueberries he'd been washing into a large bowl. He'd found several bowls in a cupboard and while she showered, he'd given the berries a good rinse and managed to find space for them in the overly large refrigerator in the kitchen.

While he'd waited for her, he'd started on some supper. He'd located some bacon in the freezer, was nuking it and was now scrambling some eggs for them. He hoped she wasn't one of those women who showered endlessly because he really was hungry.

Thankfully, within a few minutes, she padded barefoot into the kitchen, a towel wrapped around her hair and a pink flush to her skin that matched the pretty pink blouse she wore.

"You clean up nice," he blurted before he could stop himself. Heck, he needed to keep his mouth shut. But she sure did look pretty.

She averted his gaze and he realized he'd embarrassed her with his comment. Interesting. He wondered where she came from and what kind of woman would be tramping around in bear country, unescorted with buckets of blueberries. Bears loved blueberries. Maybe she had a death wish?

"Your turn. The water is nice and hot," she said as she fiddled with the coffee machine.

He shook his head and nodded to the eggs he was stirring in the pot.

"Eat first. Come on, have a seat. I'll get the coffee started and serve a fast dinner. And we can have sugared blueberries and whipped cream for dessert. Already have it waiting for us in the fridge. I figure the owners of this place won't mind us getting into their grub. They can consider it down payment for all those blueberry pies you're gonna bake for them." He winked at her and liked that her cheeks grew even pinker.

She didn't say anything. Instead she sat down on a chair, removed the towel, bent over and began to vigorously dry her hair with the towel. He watched her for a moment, mesmerized with her fingers. They were long and slender. No nail polish. Nails nicely cut and clean.

Come to think of it, she hadn't been wearing a lick of makeup when he'd found her screaming at the bear. He liked a woman who was comfortable with her own looks and didn't need makeup even out here.

Daegen quickly got the coffee brewing and then drew his attention back to stirring the eggs before they burned. He had to admit he wasn't the best of cooks, but he did whip up a fluffy batch of scrambled eggs. Mitch and Paul always looked forward to the mornings when he cooked, because they knew they'd be getting eggs. He shook in a healthy dose of salt, pepper, and the tiniest touch of some of the opened red wine he'd found in the fridge. He whipped the eggs harder and then they were done.

"Your dinner is served, my lady," Daegen said as he scooped a healthy dose of eggs onto two plates, added the cooked bacon from the microwave and set one of the plates in front of her. She'd already returned to a seated position and stared at the plate. He could tell by her growling stomach she was hungry.

As he poured coffee, he watched her dig into the food. She ate quickly and quietly except for a soft moan of appreciation that made something wild stir in Daegen. He noted her hair still wasn't dry, but it was one sexy tangled mess that he wouldn't mind combing out with his fingers. He shook his head at the stupid thought.

Okay, cut the crap, Daeg. Eat. Shower. And get to bed. Alone.

He wondered what she would think if she knew that he hadn't had sex in one hell of a long time.

"Good?" he asked as he joined her at the kitchen table. He poured coffee into her mug, then some into his too.

She nodded, wiped her mouth with the back of her hand and to his surprise, smiled. Wow. She smiled nice and the sight of her luscious lips in happy mode did some naughty things to his lower belly and parts south.

"So how long are you here for?" he asked. He had heard from Mitch that Moose Ranch had planned on hiring some woman to keep an eye on the place while the owners were away.

"Just a couple more days. I'm housesitting until they get back. I'm expecting them at any minute," she said.

He grinned inwardly. Now that seemed like a hint to him that she might be afraid of him. He needed to put her at ease.

"Doubt they'll be flying in the storm. Dangerous. Looks like you're stuck with me for the night. Or if you would rather, I can sleep out in the barn."

Her fork stopped halfway to her mouth.

Ah, so that idea had not entered her mind?

She slowly shook her head.

"You can bunk upstairs in one of the guys' rooms. I'm sure they'll have no problem with it. I can set down clean sheets for you."

He nodded and dug into his food.

Damned but he was hungry. By the time he was finished gulping it all down, he looked up to see her staring at him.

"You have a healthy appetite," she complimented.

"You too," he replied and nodded to her empty plate. "Ready for dessert?"

The lights flickered and they both stared at the lamp fixture as it dimmed to a dirty yellow, but didn't go off.

"Flashlights? Matches? Candles?" he asked.

"Top of the fridge. They have generators out back that can be turned on. They said not to wait longer than twelve hours to turn it on as the stuff in the freezers and fridge will start to spoil."

Daegen nodded as he pushed back his chair and got up.

"They're well prepared. We hope to have our place half as good by this fall."

Her head snapped up. Interest shone in her eyes.

"We?" she asked.

Was she fishing for details about a wife? He grinned inwardly as he turned and headed to the fridge to get the dessert and a flashlight. He remembered that he had told her he was gay. He figured it was best for her to continue to think that way.

"My two friends and myself. We're a few miles away down a river that comes off this lake. We're tapping into the racing horse spa business."

She got a dreamy look on her face and asked softly. "Must feel nice to live out here, all alone, being your own boss, answering to no one."

"I think you have to want this kind of life or be a certain type of person who enjoys solitude for it to work. You have to be aware that it's just you and God's country out here. That anything could go wrong and there may not be help."

She nodded and remained quiet as he set a bowl of whipping cream drenched blueberries in front of her.

"You like?" he prodded. Why had she become so silent?

She nodded again. Were those tears in her eyes? Concern gripped him.

"What's wrong? Did I ruin the blueberries in some way?" He hoped his attempt at humor might bring a smile to her face. It didn't.

He backtracked to what he'd just said that might have upset her but couldn't come up with anything.

"What I wouldn't give to be out here. Free." Her voice was so low that he had the feeling she'd left and gone somewhere else with her mind.

"Find a job with a ranch out this way. Or start a place of your own."

"I wish it was that easy, Daegen." She stuck her spoon into the whipped cream.

"It is."

"For you. Not for me."

Man, she was really down about something. He shouldn't be caring. He had too many issues of his own to deal with. He didn't need anything else on his plate. He kept quiet, not knowing what to say.

"I get the feeling that Mitch didn't tell you about me? Unless maybe Brady didn't share the news of my past."

His gut twisted with a not so good feeling. Her past?

"I'm sure it's none of my business," he stated. Suddenly the dessert wasn't tasting as good as he'd hoped.

"You rescued me from a bear. I think I owe you an explanation of who you rescued." Her voice had become soft. Outside the thunder became louder. Lightning flashed at the rain-soaked windows. It had gotten dark out there and he was glad he was here with her. That she would have spent tonight, alone, in this house, with a nasty storm, didn't sit well with him. Why would they let this woman stay here all by herself? Who was she? Some crazy antisocial lady?

"I'm actually on loan from a prison. I go back soon."

He shook his head. He didn't understand what she was saying. On loan from a prison? Like what? A prison guard?

"I'm out on a conditional leave. To see how things go. It's like a test. Some inmates get a temporary assignment while others get a permanent one right off the bat. I go back into the system and wait until another job opportunity comes up. If it's temporary, like this one, I do my job and then go back to prison until I get a permanent job. Then when I get a permanent job I can get out on parole."

"Wow, talk about an information dump." He couldn't wrap his head around what had just told him.

"Sorry," she whispered. She sounded devastated.

"You're a convict?" he said without thinking.

She scrunched up her mouth with distaste, obviously not liking that last word. But he'd said it and there was no taking it back. No use in apologizing either. He had the feeling she wouldn't believe him anyway.

"Thirteen years and counting."

"Thirteen years? Wow."

The kitchen lights flickered again. Daegen grabbed the flashlight and turned it on just as the lights went out.

Suddenly he wasn't in the mood to finish his desert.

"Talk about good timing. I guess we can have desert in the morning instead?"

She nodded and stood. "I'll put them in the fridge. I for one am ready for bed. Come on, I'll show you where you can bunk," she said.

Thirteen years. His mind was still reeling as half an hour later he was lying in one of the men's beds upstairs. It was hot inside with the windows closed. If he dared open one, even a crack it would probably rain in. So, he opted to suffer the heat.

Shit. How did a person live behind bars for thirteen years?

Yeah, it was best if he steered clear of her. He had the feeling there would be just way too much baggage between the two of them for any kind of relationship to ever work.

Daegen closed his eyes and shook his head. There he went again. Thinking crazy shit about relationships. He needed to get some sleep so he could start thinking straight.

Even as he drifted off, he knew his night would be filled with the cries and screams of his fellow soldiers and of another voice pleading for him to come home. Just like every other night.

Chapter Ten

"HE'S REALLY CUTE," JJ giggled the next evening as she and Milena took a walk after supper leaving the guys to do the dishes.

"Who's cute?" Milena laughed. She hooked elbows with JJ as they strolled out of the yard and onto the main atv trail that wound its way into the wilderness.

"Daegen, of course! You spent a night with him and you've already forgotten the hunk?"

Milena didn't answer so JJ snuck a peek at her. She had a bit of a smile on her face.

"Penny for your thoughts?" JJ prodded.

"Oh, I'm just thinking," she replied. When she didn't continue speaking, JJ shook her head. Aside from telling them that Daegen had rescued her from a bear and then returned her here during a thunderstorm in his canoe and had spent the night, she hadn't said much else about the man.

"Thinking about Daegen?" she teased.

Milena laughed.

"Well, what isn't there to think about? It's been years without a man. If he hadn't been gay I might have had a hot night with him. Instead, I slept like a rock, and in the morning, he was gone. Not even a goodbye."

JJ jolted. "Daegen? Gay? Who told you that?"

"He did."

JJ frowned. "That's weird. Why would he say that?"

"Weird why?"

"When I was in the city and Mitch and Paul stayed with me at that little apartment that belonged to the nurse, one night they told me that Daegen had had a wife. She'd died in childbirth while he'd been overseas. He'd been devastated."

Milena's hand flew to her mouth. She looked shocked and her brown eyes sparkled with tears.

"The poor man," she whispered.

There was sadness in her voice, and JJ felt bad for her. She had only seen Daegen briefly that one time when he'd brought Paul and Mitch out to the plane in that canoe when Brady had fallen ill. In her concern about Brady, JJ hadn't thought about any of the men's looks, but later, after everything had settled, she'd briefly thought that all three of them were cute.

"Maybe he told you that so you wouldn't jump his bones?" JJ teased.

"Gosh, I was too scared of him to do that. He was a stranger."

Sudden understanding burst through JJ.

"He said he was gay to put your mind at ease. He probably noticed you were afraid of him."

Milena brought them to a halt. Her mouth dropped open and she shook her head.

"I cannot believe that man. It was awfully sweet of him to put my mind at ease like that."

"Did it work?"

Milena rolled her eyes and sighed.

"Yeah. It worked. Like I said I slept like a baby."

JJ tugged her forward and they began walking again.

"Don't worry, sweetie," JJ encouraged. "You'll get your man. I'm sure of it. He will be strong and tender and sweet and caring and-"

"And now you're talking about your baby daddy," Milena said softly.

"He is adorable," JJ answered. She couldn't tell Milena that all three of her cowboys were gorgeous and she wished Milena could have three guys of her very own too.

"They are all very nice to me. I had no clue nice guys existed. Too bad I hadn't met one of them when I was a teenager. Life would have gone down a very different path," Milena said.

"Yeah, for me too. But we can't concentrate on what could have been. We have to focus on what we want and we have to work toward it," JJ replied.

Milena came to an abrupt halt and suddenly gathered JJ into her arms.

"You have come such a long way since we were together back in the pen. I am so proud of you," she whispered into JJ's ears and hugged her even tighter.

Milena's words made warmth and happiness bubble through her. JJ *had* come a long way from being the frightened, bitter woman who'd stayed in her cell as much as possible and suffered anxiety and panic attacks.

Now she had a baby on the way, was flying a plane and helping to run a cattle empire and that inner restlessness that been plaguing her since she'd hooked up with Brady, Dan and Rafe had disappeared. Life just could not get any better. She was living her dream.

Somewhere nearby from one of the treetops an owl hooted and Milena let go of JJ. Then she hooked her arm with hers again and they began walking once more. Milena's gaze was all over the place as they both tried to locate the owl who kept hooting.

"I love that sound. It's spooky but it sounds like freedom. This whole untamed place with such rich colors of green trees, sparkling blue lakes and crazy creatures, touches emotions inside of me that I never knew I had. Do you know what I mean?" she asked.

JJ nodded. "It's freedom. Some call it getting back to nature. Or tapping into their wild side. Tomorrow we're taking the entire day off for ourselves. I'm going to take you up into the sky and show you more of the wilderness. I know you flew in with Blue, so she was on her best flying behaviour. But flying with me is a whole different ball game. We can go over to see the cabin that the guys built too. We'll have a picnic there. How's that sound?"

Milena brightened. "I'd like that."

"Great! Now let's get a move on. We've got one hour left of light and I say let's take full advantage of working off the supper we just had."

Her friend nodded and before JJ knew it, they were walking so fast, it felt as if she was flying and she loved it.

"Lake Nipigon is so beautiful, JJ. Thank you for bringing me here. I absolutely love the way it sparkles beneath the sunlight."

"I thought you might like it," JJ replied, as the next day, she flew her plane over the largest lake within the boundaries of Ontario.

JJ smiled as Milena kept her eager gaze focused out the window and her hands clutched to her chest in awe. For a long time, they were quiet as she flew them over numerous square shaped table top islands with their spectacular sheer cliffs and black sandy beaches.

JJ wondered how she could ever have lived without flying a plane or seeing the earth from this vantage. Maybe that was why she had had such a run of bad luck for so many years? She hoped that God had been saving up to get her a real happy ever after.

She dropped the plane lower so they could get a closer look at the sparkling waters and the towering tree tops.

"Wow, I feel like I can just reach out and grab those branches," Milena whispered dreamily.

"Why don't you learn how to fly? If I can do it, anyone can."

Milena grinned and shook her head.

"I would rather be the passenger. It is so much less stressful. Besides, I doubt I will get as lucky as you. No one worth their marbles is gonna take a chance on hiring me if they find out I am a convict."

JJ frowned.

"But we took a chance on you," she said softly.

Milena swore softly and faced JJ. She looked horrified.

"Oh gosh! I am so sorry. I didn't mean you guys. I really stuck my foot in my mouth."

"Don't worry about it. I just wanted to remind you that you are worth something. There are kind hearted people around and someone will want to take a chance on you. I know Jenna is working hard for women and men like us. She came through for me and she will come through for you too."

JJ gazed at the clock on the dash. It was getting late.

"Oops, time to start back," JJ stated.

"Bummer. It is so pretty here."

"I guess you are as addicted to nature as I am."

Milena laughed.

"Now that's one kind of addiction that's good for your health."

As JJ angled the plane back around, she dropped even lower so they could get a better look at the sheer cliffs on some of the islands and at the sparkling sandy beaches.

Her instructor, Kaley, had brought her here last year and JJ had remembered Milena once mentioning how much she loved islands. Her friend had gotten an eyeful today.

They fell silent again for a long time. The picturesque view was relaxing and quite mesmerizing.

"Do you really think I will get out of prison permanently?" Milena suddenly asked. "I mean I have more than ten years left on my sentence. Why would they let me out early?"

"Prisons are overcrowded. They are looking for ways to release people. Programs are available. Besides, they wouldn't let you out temporarily if they didn't have some amount of trust in you to come back, right? You're not violent. You aren't a threat to others. You're clean of drugs. Consider it as a test."

"I guess," she whispered.

Man, Milena's confidence *had* taken a pounding since their prison time together. They fell silent again as the giant lake disappeared behind them. The low rumble of the engine relaxed JJ and she flew them low so they could catch glimpses of the waterfalls and rapids along the meandering Nipigon river as it wove its way through the forest. After awhile she veered away from the river and headed east to head back toward the ranch property.

It would be another half an hour before they reached the lake with the newly built cabin and JJ was glad when Milena suggested they have lunch. She hadn't realized she was hungry but yeah, she suddenly was famished.

Milena poured hot coffee and while they drank, they also ate the roast beef sandwiches that Dan had packed for them this morning. They chatted about the animals that lived in the forest and when Milena asked her about the head-stomping moose and man-eating beavers that Daegen had mentioned, JJ laughed.

She laughed so hard, she could barely see out the window from the tears that blurred her vision.

"Why in the world would he say those things if it wasn't true?" Milena asked with a frown after JJ calmed enough to tell her that Daegen had been teasing her.

JJ shook her head and bit her lip to keep from laughing some more.

"Was he making fun of me?"

"Probably thought you were a city girl. Perhaps he just has a twisted sense of humor? Or maybe he was trying to scare you into not wandering into the woods alone again? Hmm, maybe I should have done that. Obviously my approach didn't work with you. That bear could have killed you."

Guilt flashed in Milena's eyes. "Sorry, but I was seriously going bat-shit stir crazy with no one to talk to."

"I bake when I have no company. Or I tend to the garden. Or I go swimming in the lake. Lots of things to do."

"What about winter? Are the men gone for long periods of time in the winter?"

"They usually come home for supper. Cattle still have to be fed out in the meadows, so in the winter we fly out the food for them and drop the bales and other food out of the plane as we fly over. But before we got the plane, I was alone all the time my first winter because they took the hay out on snowmobiles with trailers. It was crazy rough work. Much easier and so fast with a plane."

"Wow, what would they do without you, JJ?" Milena mused. She wiped some mustard off her mouth with a napkin.

"They managed before I came along. But I'm glad I can help. It makes me feel useful."

"I hear you. Now that I've had a taste of freedom, I think maybe my next time on the outside I'll appreciate my alone time." Milena replied.

JJ grinned. Maybe a lesson had been learned for her old friend?

"That was an awfully good sandwich. Want desert? Dan packed us some of those blueberry muffins we made last night," Milena said.

JJ's mouth watered.

"Sure! And another cup of coffee, if you please."

Milena poured her another cup, dropped in some sugar cubes and a couple of teaspoons of powdered coffee whitener and stirred. JJ accepted the steaming drink and set it into her cup holder and then eagerly took the offered blueberry muffin. They nibbled on dessert and renewed their conversation about the animals who lived in the forest below.

"Okay, so here's the scoop on the animal life. We have wolves, coyotes, deer and black bears. Daegen was right about you need to make noise so they can run away. I should have told you but well, I thought you wouldn't go into the woods. Anyways, moose. Yes, moose can be dangerous. They have long legs that can swivel and hit you if you get too close and you scare them. Some moose are pretty territorial and have been known to attack humans. The same goes with bears. Beavers can attack you too if they have their babies around."

"Gosh, it all sounds dangerous."

"The trick is to make noise. Hit a stick against a tree, blow a whistle once in a while or just sing. As long as they know you're around, chances are they'll stay out of the way."

"Sounds easy enough."

"Do we have any more of those muffins?" JJ asked with a chuckle. She still couldn't believe how mean Daegen could be to poor Milena. But she was sure he had his reasons.

Milena laughed. "The muffins are good, aren't they?"

"Yes, we have four more. Want another one?"

JJ was just about to say yes, when a blinking red warning light on the dashboard caught her attention.

She tensed and she gazed at the oil gauge. The oil was low. Too low. *What in the world?*

She had done a safety check just before leaving this morning. The oil had been almost full. A whisper of smoke drifted out of the engine area.

Shit! A leak?

Panic snapped through JJ, but she forced herself to try and think. Her mind remained a stubborn blank. Her anxiety mounted.

Low oil. Smoke.

They were in trouble.

"JJ? Do you want another muffin?" Milena asked.

"Milena. I don't want you to panic, but I've got to make an emergency call."

Milena gasped and looked around the cockpit.

"What? What's wrong?"

JJ ignored her and reached for the radio. It took her longer than usual to get a connection and when she managed to hail traffic control and relayed her coordinates stating she had engine trouble and that she needed help, the answering connection crackled. She thought she heard someone acknowledge what she'd said, but she couldn't be sure.

The engine sputtered. The smoke grew denser.

"Oh my God! JJ! There's smoke!" Milena shouted and pointed out the front window.

"I know. We'll be okay."

Yeah, right.

She could take the plane higher and get above the surrounding hills to get a better connection and send out another distress call, but instincts told her it was best to land right away.

"JJ, are we going to crash?"

JJ's panic rose. She fought it off.

"Not if I can help it. I did not come this far to have it all taken away from me."

"Can I do something to help?"

JJ gazed over at her friend.

"Get into the position I showed you before we took flight. Do you remember my emergency instructions?"

Milena jerkily nodded. Fear brightened her eyes.

She snapped on her seat belt, bent forward and dipped hear down between her knees.

"Good. Stay there."

JJ strapped on her seat belt, making sure it was tucked safely beneath her baby bump.

Don't worry, sweetheart, she silently whispered to her baby. *We will get through this. We have to.*

Until just a few moments ago, she thought her plane was her best friend, but now she felt betrayed.

The plane shuddered. Instinct told her the plane was going to stall.

She wondered if she should pray? Like she did when Brady had fallen ill. Would God listen to her again? Would he think she was greedy asking for his help again? Just thinking about how Brady had gotten better, renewed her faith that everything was going to work out okay. Suddenly all her panic vanished. She began to calm. If not a lake, then a meadow. There had to be a meadow somewhere.

There has to be something.

"Brace yourself, Milena. I'm taking it down," JJ replied.

"Oh my God! Where can we land? There's only trees down there!" Milena cried. Thankfully she remained in her position.

"I just need to find a lake or a meadow," JJ said with a coolness that she should not be feeling under the circumstances. Was she in shock? The baby picked that moment to punch her tummy.

Sorry for the stress, kid. She resisted the urge to smooth her hand over her belly and soothe her baby.

"Can we turn back? Land in Nipigon Lake?"

"No, it's more than an hour back now. Too far. No time."

The baby kicked again. Harder this time, as if knowing they were in a dire situation.

The engine sputtered. Then stalled.

Oh, damn!

Hunger and weariness tugged at Rafe as he brought the tractor into the yard. He'd been haying all day in the meadows closest to the ranch and he couldn't wait to feast his eyes on JJ, have a good meal, talk with everyone about what he'd got done and then just relax. Maybe play cards with Milena. She was a pretty good card player. He figured one got to be good at card games with being locked behind bars for so many years.

His thoughts disintegrated the instant he spied Brady and Dan rush out of the ranch house. As they hurried toward him, both men were frantically waving their arms at him to stop right then and there. Alarm raced through him and when he switched off the tractor he was already praying like crazy that they weren't freaking out because of something happening to JJ and the baby.

"Did JJ tell you where she and Milena were going today?" Brady asked in a too-loud voice that spelled trouble. When he was upset, he was impatient. When he was upset about anything to do with JJ, he was brash.

"No. I haven't seen her since after breakfast. She mentioned last night she was taking the morning and afternoon off and taking Milena up with the plane, remember? They were heading out to the new shelter and then some sightseeing around the perimeter of the land and maybe taking a dash over to show Milena Lake Nipigon but not necessarily in that order. I don't remember her saying of going anywhere else. She said they would be back to get supper on for us. Why?"

"The girls are missing. No note. No plane. No supper. No JJ. Where the fuck are they?" Brady hissed as he stared in the direction of the dock. Rafe followed his gaze. There was no white plane moored there.

Damn.

"She would be humming over a pot of something about now. You know how she loves to stick to her routine," Dan said.

"Where the hell is she?" Brady growled. He shoved his hands through his hair in obvious frustration. If Rafe didn't know any better, he would think Brady was about to lose it and sink into a state of panic.

Brady continued, his words coming out in a rush, just like a confession.

"I've had a really bad feeling for a long time about her flying. Even had nightmares. Like a premonition or something. I just knew something like this was going to happen. I just fucking *knew* it."

"Okay, okay, maybe she sent out a distress call. Have you checked with the authorities?" Rafe asked as he joined Dan and Brady who were headed back to the ranch house.

Both men said no because they had just gotten back themselves.

"So exactly how long has JJ been missing?" Dan asked as they stepped into the building.

No one answered.

Rafe tried to keep calm, but all kinds of bad scenarios were rolling around in his head. There should be the smells of a succulent supper drifting through the air. Instead, there was just the familiar scent of the natural pine they'd used to make their furniture.

"That fucking radio of hers doesn't work that great, remember? Kaley mentioned it should be fixed when we bought the plane off her," Brady huffed as he got out the address book, whipped it open and started pressing numbers on the phone.

"I believe she did that the first time she went into Thunder Bay when she started flying solo. I remember seeing the repair bill on the desk last fall," Dan said.

Brady nodded. "Okay, yes, I remember now. You're right."

Then he began speaking in the phone to someone.

Rafe's gaze flew to Dan. He was biting his bottom lip and staring at Brady. Rafe drew his attention to study Brady's face too, searching for any indication of good or bad news.

It took fifteen minutes of run around calls to different departments before Brady got an answer. His face had paled significantly and Rafe braced himself for the bad news.

"Yes, a distress call did come in. Co-ordinates were given but the pilot stated an engine problem and they weren't sure the entire message was delivered. A rescue plane was sent to the area and have been unable to locate any plane...or any debris. They are calling off the search due the light failing. They plan on resuming tomorrow whenever the weather clears. They said there is another storm coming tonight." Brady spoke in the calmest voice Rafe had ever heard from him.

Debris as in plane crash. Calling off the search as in the girls are stuck out there in the forest or wherever they might be for the night. This late in August it got cold at night. JJ would need to keep herself warm...because of the baby.

Rafe's gut hollowed out and for a moment he couldn't breathe. He felt as if he'd been sucker-punched.

Beside him, Dan swore.

"What are the co-ordinates?" Rafe asked as he rushed into the living room to the corner cabinet where they kept the topographical maps.

Brady read out the co-ordinates JJ had given with her distress call.

Rafe knew the area. It was several miles north of the new shelter in some of the densest forest with plenty of rocky hills, towering pines and gorges. It was not a good place to go down in an emergency especially since there weren't any lakes out in that area. He also knew that when a pilot sent out an incomplete distress call, the plane could travel many miles, if the problem wasn't serious. He held out hope it wasn't too serious. To think of any alternative, all bad, would simply send his mind spiralling into madness.

"I'll get some grub and water for us," Brady growled as he began grabbing dried food items from cupboards and placing them on the dining table.

Rafe looked at Dan, who shrugged and shook his head.

"There's no way I'm sitting around waiting for some search party to return to looking," he continued. "If the plane has gone down, they need help now. I need to be out looking for her and not waiting around here. Shit! Now I understand how she feels when she says she can't stay here when one of us is in trouble,"

Rafe placed the topographical map onto the kitchen table and both he and Dan studied the map.

"You and I can get to the area via the motorboat," Rafe suggested to Dan as he ran a finger along a river system. "We'll tow a canoe behind the boat and then start portaging into the river system. There are several rivers in that area. They'll be easier to travel than through the bush."

"Hey, man. I'm going too," Brady called out. "My legs might not be all there, but I can still hoof it as good as you guys."

Rafe knew Brady believed he could do it, but Rafe knew better. He caught Dan's slight shake of his head.

"I'm wondering if maybe you should head up to the new cabin with an all terrain vehicle, in case she headed back there? She may or may not stay with the plane. We should cover all our bases," Rafe suggested to Brady.

He didn't want to tell Brady outright that he would only slow them down during portages and when they left the canoe and travelled into the dense wilderness on foot. Truth be told, he didn't want Brady with them in case there'd been a crash.

Brady frowned. Was he picking up on the hint?

"We haven't outfitted a sat phone at that cabin yet. She left her phone here," He pointed to the phone set on a kitchen chair. "If they do get there and decide to use the all terrain vehicles on site, on the trail at night, with her not being experienced with night driving..." Dan added slowly.

"Fine," Brady huffed. "I will go out there. But we stay in touch via sat phone at every hour. Top of the hour."

Rafe nodded. "Okay. Dan pack the maps and help Brady with getting grub for us. Brady, bring a first aid kit with you too. Just in case. Dan, I'll get a sat phone, extra fuel for the motor, and first aid kit and meet you down at the boat."

God help them, he hoped the emergency supplies would not be needed.

Chapter Eleven

"ARE YOU SURE YOU'RE all right?" Milena asked JJ as they trudged through the dense underbrush. JJ led the way, with Milena holding her hand. It was dark and the ground was tricky to maneuver with fallen logs to step over and branches that slapped against their faces. The only form of light was a small flashlight that she kept in the plane. She also had an emergency box of waterproof matches, candles, some flint, dry food such as raisins, peanuts, instant soups, chocolate bars and a couple of bottles of water in her emergency pack.

She was also very grateful she kept a compass and detailed map that Dan had given her after they'd purchased the plane. He'd instructed her on how to use those items. He had told her to keep them in her pack. Just in case, he'd said. Map and compass were coming in very handy now.

"I'm okay. A bit roughed up. But baby is sleeping soundly." Truth of the matter was when she'd glided the plane down, the left pontoon had snapped off the top of a towering pine tree as they'd glided into the small meadow she'd spied at the last minute. It had turned the plane and set her onto a path she hadn't wanted to go on. So, it had been a very rough landing as the wheels beneath the pontoon hadn't liked the tall tangled grass and overgrown bushes. They'd both been jostled against their seat belts and she was experiencing some lower back discomfort. She prayed the baby was okay.

She knew it was protocol to stay with the plane during an emergency, but after a quick engine check she realized parts were needed. Luckily the pontoon had only suffered a mild dent. The wheels appeared to be okay but she couldn't be sure a hundred percent.

There hadn't been any safe area in the overgrown meadow to build a fire to stay warm for the night. She'd left the emergency locator on in the plane when they'd left it, and she'd etched cuts out of the bark of trees with her small jackknife every twenty or so feet until they hit the river. When someone found the plane, they could follow them.

She'd decided it best they keep moving to stay warm and follow a river they'd found using the map. According to map and compass this river would eventually lead them to the lake with the new cabin. She continued to hope, perhaps naively, they would find a suitable area for a campfire along the river, but nothing yet.

Milena had fallen silent and JJ noticed the wind was picking up. They were warm enough with extra clothing, thermal underwear, and wool hats that she kept in the plane, but trudging through this forest brought back memories of the stormy morning when they'd gone in to rescue Brady.

"How about you? Are you cold?" JJ asked, keeping the conversation going. She'd rather talk than listen to the branches cracking overhead.

"My hands and feet are a bit chilled, but I can handle it. I don't need that pocket warmer yet."

JJ had the pocket warmer in the knapsack and had wanted Milena to use it as JJ wore the only pair of warm gloves. She'd offered to take turns with the gloves with Milena, but she had refused them and the pocket warmer citing JJ needed to stay warm for the baby's sake.

"It's starting to rain," Milena whispered in a strangled voice.

No!

Sure enough as JJ lifted her face upward, cold drops of water dripped against her skin.

Her enthusiasm for getting out of this predicament without too much difficulty shorted out. Had they stayed with the plane, they would have at least been dry. She had only one small raincoat in the emergency pack. One of them was going to get very cold and very fast if the rain picked up.

JJ's heart plummeted as lightning flickered through the canopy of trees.

Oh no! She'd screwed up. They should have stayed with the plane. Now they were going to pay for her stupidity.

Rafe and Dan paddled as best they could along the wide river through the darkness. They'd strapped a battery-operated spotlight to the front of the canoe and that allowed them to see a short distance ahead. The river they'd picked was deep and ran directly along the co-ordinates JJ had given the authorities. She could have veered off to the right or to the left and be miles off, but when one was looking for a needle in a haystack, so to speak, one had to start somewhere.

"She should have taken her satellite phone with her. That would have solved a lot of problems," Rafe grumbled angrily from the seat in front of Dan.

"She probably forgot it there with all that was going on," Dan replied, trying to protect JJ. But Rafe was right. JJ was the one who was always calling out to them before they left for work to make sure they had their phones on them in case of an emergency.

"Make sure you have your sat phone? Did you pack your sat phone? Let me see it, just to make sure," she'd say. Her eyes would glisten happily when one or all of them would show her their phones.

She was like a mother hen, always reminding them. Then what does she go and do? Forgets her damn phone. The girls had probably been chatting and excited to go out and JJ hadn't picked it up.

"JJ, baby, you are so going to pay for this," Dan mumbled.

He watched Rafe reach down for the blow horn. Brady had bought the item at an auction sale in Thunder Bay the first year they'd been on the ranch. Back then there hadn't been a ranch house. They had had just a tent, an open pit for a fireplace to cook on and a forest full of bears that came too close for comfort. They'd gotten tired of bear steak pretty quick and Brady stated the blow horn would come in useful to scare away bears. It had.

Hopefully it would come in useful this time with JJ.

"JJ! Jennifer Jane! Milena!" Rafe shouted through the horn.

Dan wasn't sure if JJ or Milena heard and then responded, that they would even hear them with the water splashing against the side of the aluminum canoe, the rush of the wind through the branches and now thunder grumbling somewhere off in the distance.

Man! Could this scenario get any worse? It was a good thing this hadn't happened in calving season, Dan thought as he stopped paddling while Rafe called out again. He knew they would all still have come out in search for her, but the added burden of not being there to help the cows give birth would have weighed on them. But JJ was top priority. She would always take precedence now over everything. JJ and the baby.

His gut clenched at the thought of losing both or one. And what about Milena? Locked up for so many years only to get out and then die in a plane crash.

They'd been paddling now for hours. In another couple of hours, it would be daybreak and the professional search plane would be sent out again, if weather permitted.

Desperation grabbed at Dan. What if they were never found? Bush planes went down in this vast wilderness every year. Most were found. Some people alive...some dead...yet some...were never found.

Rafe inhaled a shuddering, slow breath and forced his thoughts away from visions of a violent crash. JJ was a good pilot. Hell, hadn't she brought down that plane on small lakes without a problem? She'd been taught by the best pilot too.

They would find JJ and Milena. They had to. There was no other option.

"Still no sign of them?" Brady repeated what Dan had just told him over the sat phone. The sun was up now and Brady still hadn't been able to reach the new cabin. With the overnight wind, a couple of trees had come down over the trail and he'd had to chainsaw with hands that still didn't work one hundred percent. With the rain, the trail had gotten muddy in spots making it hard to maneuver the machine, slowing him down some.

"Sorry," Dan said. "We've been in touch with search and rescue and they've sent two planes out and are doing a grid search. One to the south of us and the other to the north of the new cabin. Stay in that area. She might even go for the railroad to flag down the engineer. She has a compass and a map."

Brady could barely hear him, even with the engine shut off. Had he said she had a compass and a map? Or had that been wishful thinking? The connection crackled, the wind was blowing like a bitch and it was creating a chill in him. He needed to get to the new cabin, get warmed up and start looking at the other shelters and the railroad.

He had no doubt that JJ, if she had survived a crash, and was able to move, would have left the plane to search for appropriate shelter so they could stay warm. The forested area north of their ranch was so dense, that the smallest fire in an inappropriate spot could start a forest fire. Even after last night's rain, he knew the warm sun would quickly dry up the trail and woods.

Brady shuddered at the thought of a crash and tried to focus on JJ and the baby and Milena being okay.

He didn't want to imagine JJ being injured and trapped in the tangled wreckage of the plane. Couldn't even bring himself to think about what might have happened to his baby. Didn't want to contemplate that both women and his baby might be dead. But those thoughts hounded him like the devil itself. That creepy feeling that had been haunting him for months of something happening with JJ because of that damned plane, hadn't been some sort of anxiety shit. It had been a premonition. A warning that he should have acted upon.

"I'm almost at the north cabin. Talk next hour. Over and out." Brady waited for a reply, but none came. He holstered his phone and started the machine. When he got his hands on his woman, he swore he was going to make sure she *never* left that ranch house ever again even if he had to tie her to his bed!

Brady stared at the smoke uncurling from the chimney in the new cabin as he stood outside beside the atv. He'd been here about an hour now. He'd changed clothing. Cooked up some food, not that he was hungry, but he needed to feed himself in order to stay healthy. He knew he should lie down and rest his stiff, painful legs and get some sleep, but he needed to get back out on the trails. Needed to keep looking.

He settled his helmet onto his head and was about to start the atv when something in the nearby forest caught his eye. A flash of black. Bear? Oh crap, that was the last thing he needed right now. He heard a stick crack. Saw movement.

Definitely some animal in the forest. He waited. Maybe it would just pass by? Or maybe it was hostile and hungry?

Slowly, he strolled to the trailer attached to the atv. He kept his rifle there. It was fully loaded but with the safety on. Being out in the wilderness, unarmed, was not a good idea. He took his attention off the movement to unlatch the rope that held his plastic-wrapped rifle. Then he pulled out his weapon, raised it and waited.

Two figures stumbled out of the woods. At first, he thought he must have fallen asleep and was dreaming.

But when they waved to him, he could only stand there and shake his head with shock. And then reality crashed through him and he was running.

JJ swore she had never been hugged so hard than when Brady grabbed her and lifted her off her feet, twirling her around as if she was a rag doll. She winced as her sore back spasmed, but as he rained hot kisses all over her face, the pain was forgotten.

"Good God! You are all right. I cannot believe it!" he shouted. He settled her on her feet and stared at her with the biggest smile she'd ever seen.

"Sorry, I caused you guys to worry," JJ whispered. Emotions overwhelmed her. Happiness that their misadventure was finally over. Guilt for causing them to worry and for endangering their baby.

Tears sprang up, blinding her from seeing Brady. Her lower lip and chin went into a mad uncontrollable tremble.

"I'm so sorry. So very sorry," she sobbed.

"You guys are okay. There is nothing to be sorry about, baby," he murmured.

His palm curled around hers and he squeezed reassuringly. She suddenly felt safe.

"The baby?" he asked as he led them to the cabin.

"We hit the ground really hard. She should be checked out by a doctor," JJ heard Milena say.

"I'll make the arrangements right after I make you both a very hot and hearty meal. Are your clothes wet?"

"Milena's are. She made me wear this raincoat. Black is not my color."

To her surprise, Brady laughed.

"I thought you were a bear. Had the rifle all ready to go. I was just about to leave and keep looking for you," Brady said as he ushered them into the toasty cabin.

"There's extra clothing in the back room on one of the bunks. Men's clothing, but warm. Off with the two of you, then come back and sit in front of the fireplace. I have stew with bear steak ready when you get out."

JJ nodded. She led Milena into the bunkroom and wiped away her tears. It was cool back here, but everything looked just the way they had left it when the four of them had stayed here their last night and she had tidied up the morning before they'd left.

"He sure was glad to see you," Milena chuckled as she began to undress. "I want a man who loves me just like Brady loves you. Do you think it's possible?"

"Hey, girlfriend. If I can find love here in the middle of nowhere then you can too. It's in the stars for us. Now let's get out of these sweaty, damp clothes and grab some grub. I'm starving."

She wanted to see Brady again. Wanted to be with him. To tell him how much she loved him. Then she wanted to kiss Rafe and Dan like they'd never been kissed before. How she'd missed all three of them last night.

Her tummy growled.

She hoped that being hungry was a good sign. She smiled as she felt a butterfly kick against her abdomen. It seemed baby was okay too. Silently she sent up a huge prayer of thanks for all three of them making it back out alive.

The next couple of days flew by so quickly, that JJ couldn't believe Milena was about to fly away in the blue plane with Blue. Earlier this morning, Blue had flown in a doctor who made house-calls.

JJ had already been on the phone with the remote bush doctor whom Blue had suggested when she heard about the accident. After answering all of Dr. Marley Jensen's questions, the doctor had advised JJ to lay in bed until she could get out to see her. Paul had called too asking questions about the crash and if she had any symptoms. He'd also suggested bed rest.

So, JJ had spent Milena's last two days of freedom in bed. Milena had doted on her and cooked meals for JJ's men following JJ's instructions. Milena had done a very good job, but JJ was itching to get out bed.

Relief poured through her when her doctor arrived. After a thorough examination, Dr. Jensen had stated the baby was fine and the tense muscles in her lower back was due to a strain from the accident. The doctor had also said had JJ not been wearing her seatbelt correctly, things would not have turned out well for the baby. She'd given JJ some light physiotherapy exercises.

The doctor was now in the plane with Blue, awaiting Milena to board.

JJ had asked the guys to say their goodbyes to Milena after breakfast. They'd been so sweet in hugging her during the farewell. They'd even surprised Milena with a framed picture of the ranch house so she would remember that she was always welcome here. A bank account had been opened in her name and her pay from ranch sitting would be waiting for her when she got out of prison and had access.

JJ had managed to keep her emotions together as she helped Milena hurriedly pack.

She'd thought she would be strong when she said goodbye to her old prison friend, but on the way down to the lake, seeing Blue's floatplane moored at the dock, JJ lost it and started sobbing uncontrollably.

Then Milena had joined her. They'd held onto each other as they'd walked down. Then they'd hugged in the brisk August breeze. When Milena let go of her, JJ was surprised when Milena handed her a thumb sized sparkling gold rock.

"I know it's not real gold, but it reminded me of you, JJ. I found it during that walk out to get the blueberries and stuffed it into my pocket. You are precious just like gold. You are tough and beautiful. I want you to think of me whenever you look at this rock. Remember me, JJ because I will never forget you. The first chance I get, I'll come and visit."

JJ choked back a sob, nodded and accepted the rock. It glittered in the sunlight and already made her feel a bit better.

Then Milena ducked under the wing, stepped onto the pontoon and climbed into the plane.

JJ spied the doctor at one of the window seats, her smile was caring and gentle. Then she saw Milena's pale face in a window behind the doctor as she took her seat. Tears flashed in the sunlight as they streamed down Milena's cheeks. The plane roared to life and Milena waved goodbye.

And then she was gone. As if she'd just been a dream.

JJ inhaled a shuddering breath as she watched the bright bush plane disappear into the blue distance.

She prayed that they would meet again. Prayed that Jenna would find a suitable and permanent placement for her friend.

After a few minutes of sobbing, JJ bit her bottom lip and forced herself to steady her breathing. Okay, she needed to pull herself together and get back into her routine. She needed to distract herself from the pain of loss that was hugging her.

She'd gotten close to Milena again and now it felt as if her heart was ripping apart in much the same way it had that morning when she'd learned that Milena had been transferred to another prison.

JJ gazed at the empty space by the dock where her plane should be moored. She wished she could go up and fly. To be free and to forget.

She always felt so good soaring into the sky. But the plane was still out in that small meadow. Thankfully Kaley was coming next week to fly JJ to the area where she'd downed the plane. After explaining to her ex-flight instructor what had happened, Kaley said she suspected that she knew what the problem could be. She would bring out the appropriate parts and show JJ how to take them out and put in the new ones. She would also do a thorough inspection of the pontoons and wheels.

Until then, she was grounded. She wished she could stay here and feel sorry for herself and fully embrace the hurt she felt for Milena having to go back to prison. She knew it was torture for her friend. It had to be.

But JJ didn't want to make herself sadder than she already felt with Milena's departure. The sun was shining, the air was warm and fresh, and she wished she could stay down here and absorb the beauty of the shimmering lake waters. But there were so many chores to catch up on. She had a ranch to run and she'd best get to it.

Protectively she cradled her belly as she walked up the trail.

"Baby girl or baby boy, you are going to be so happy here. You'll have three dads and they all love you so much," she said softly under her breath. She laughed as the baby gave her a swift kick.

"I cannot wait to meet you, sweetheart. I already love you so much that I swear if anything had happened to you during that crash, I would have died." And she meant it.

Another kick. This one was gentle as if the baby was trying to sooth JJ. It worked.

She smiled and stepped up the stairs to the back door of the ranch house. She let herself into the mudroom, suddenly eager to get started on preparing dinner for the guys. A nice pot roast, drenched in onions, carrots, and herbs from the garden would be perfect. She would let the roast simmer slowly all afternoon in the crock pot and it would be ready just in time for supper. And then after they ate they could indulge in dessert. Sex.

She chuckled at that thought. The four of them hadn't been together since that last night at the new cabin. Stormy storm sex it had been. She blew out a tense breath as she remembered that night.

The men's faces flushed with desire. Her cries as they thrust into her.

The pleasure, the orgasms. Their tender lovemaking.

Okay, calm down, JJ. Keep your mind on the job. Sex tonight. Plenty of sex tonight.

She nodded and when she entered the kitchen, she abruptly stopped.

Dan, Rafe and Brady were right there in her kitchen. All three stood in a straight line, facing her. They were fully dressed in their work clothing, wore their cowboy hats and oh boy did they ever look sexy.

"I thought you guys were catching up on work today. You aren't supposed to be back until supper," she teased. She was *so* glad they had come back early.

"We've been away from you for too damn many nights. Now with Milena on her way—" Brady was cut off by Rafe.

"Not that we didn't like having her around—"

Dan cut off Rafe.

"We did. She's a very nice lady. But we missed you like crazy, baby. You know we can't make love to you when someone is in the house."

"Too noisy, are you boys?" she teased.

"Us? Noisy?" Brady chuckled.

"Baby girl, you're the one who can't keep quiet and that's exactly the way we want you," Rafe muttered as he began unbuckling his belt.

"Yeah, sweetness," Dan whispered. He unzipped his jeans. "We like you nice and loud."

"Why don't you make me nice and loud, boys?" she breathed. "But first, why not take this outdoors. Into the sunshine. Let's show nature how it's really done."

Brady groaned as he got her meaning.

"You want outdoor sex? We'll give you outdoor sex."

JJ giggled and she watched as all three men began removing their pants. She waited until their pants were almost off before making her move.

"But you'll have to catch me first. While I'm skinny dipping!" she shouted as she ran for the back door.

By the time she reached the dock, she had her top and bra off. At the end of the dock, she kicked off her shoes, tore off her socks, and pulled down her shorts and panties. She heard the three of them laughing as they stomped onto the dock behind her.

JJ jumped into the lake. She closed her eyes and hit the water with a giant splash. The cool liquid embraced her and JJ wasted no time in spreading out her arms and kicking her feet while staying underwater. She swam away from the dock.

Man! Swimming was the best, almost as freeing as flying. But swimming in the nude was even better.

She stayed under the water for as long as she safely dared, doing the breaststroke, and kicking her feet. When she popped her head above water and sucked in the fresh air, she gazed around. None of the guys was anywhere in sight! But she spied all three cowboy hats had been set in a line along the edge of the dock.

She grinned. Were they playing hide and seek? Did they expect her to get out of the water, naked, and start searching the nearby woods for them? If so, they would have a long wait. She was going to swim and wait until they came back.

For a moment, she thought about Milena and a sharp blade of loss twisted through her. Milena would be feeling very bad now. But JJ hoped and prayed Jenna would find some nice home for her as she had for JJ.

She flipped over onto her back and started to float, forcing thoughts of Milena from her mind. She didn't want to think about what her friend was going back to. Didn't want to think at all about anything. Maybe she was being selfish not wanting to feel the hurt. Or maybe she just wanted to be happy.

She gazed down at her plump breasts and ultra-big nipples and then at her large baby bump. She liked what she saw. By Christmas she was going to be a mother and for some insane reason, she felt confident that she would be a good mom, despite her anxiety issues.

She looked up as she leisurely moved her arms and legs through the water. Above her, the sky was clear and blue and she watched a little blue dragonfly sweep back and forth a few inches from her face. Suddenly the dragonfly flew off as first one, then another and then a third figure erupted from the water in a semi-circle around her. Gasps of breaths and amused male chuckles surrounded her.

Dan. Rafe. And Brady! She struggled to turn over and swim away. But she was too late! JJ screamed as a hand slid beneath her waist, keeping her firmly on her back and floating. She knew the water this far from the dock was mid-chest deep. So, she really had no fear that if Dan suddenly let her go that she would sink under the water. If she wasn't fast enough to swim in her awkward condition due to the baby, her feet would quickly touch the sandy bottom.

"Easy, hon. I won't let you go," Dan said from her left side as he stared down at her. His green eyes sparkled with arousal. Droplets of water streamed off his light brown hair and beaded over his face and his lips. He smiled and her heart did a wonderful pitter patter. My gosh, he looked adorable with a shadow of facial hair and heavy-lidded lust-filled eyes.

"Thought you guys had gone back to work," she teased as she squirmed against him.

"You're our work today, sweetheart. And I mean that in the utmost pleasurable way," Rafe said from her right side.

Her gaze drew to him. He had *that* look on his face. One that she recognized as a man who desired her. His dark brown eyes glittered with a promise of good things to come and her breath caught at the sudden longing for sex moving like a whirlwind through her.

"Working hard to pleasure you, baby momma," Brady added from down by her feet. Sparkles of water shone in his brown hair and he watched her like a predatory animal who knew what he wanted, and he wanted *her*. Today his eyes were the same color as the sky. Cheerful blue. He winked at her and then he spoke to Dan.

"Go ahead and kiss her. You got to her first. That was our agreement."

JJ laughed. "What are you saying?"

"First one who got to you, gets the first kiss," Rafe stated.

She looked at him and noted the beads of water sparkling on his eyelashes and glistening on the stubble of beard that hugged his chin and cheeks. Such a sexy man.

My man. My men.

"And I have no say in the matter?" she asked, suddenly feeling breathless and helpless.

All the men shook their heads.

"None. You are at our total mercy for the rest of the day," Dan replied.

She trembled with excitement. "I do like the sound of that. I wonder what getting to me second and third meant?"

Dan wiggled his eyebrows. "You'll find out."

Oh.

She inhaled as Rafe's strong hands slid under her upper back. He held her level with the water, giving all three men an up close and personal view of her breasts, baby bump and pussy.

She noticed the men were licking their lips with anticipation. Her breath caught as she began to understand what they had planned.

Brady gently pulled apart her legs and he stepped in between them. Her pussy grew hot. The lapping of water caressing her clit created a heavy intense ache deep inside of her vagina. Brady's gaze darkened with carnal intent. He slipped his hands on each side of her hips, bracing her.

Her heart thumped out of control as Dan dipped his head toward her face. He parted his lips.

JJ closed her eyes and Dan's hot mouth melted over hers, rocking her senses with an exploding kiss. Her entire body tightened with awareness as his lips stroked hers, first gently and then demanding. She lifted her right arm and curled it over his neck bringing him closer and deeper into the kiss. Electrical arcs zipped through her.

She moaned as Rafe's mouth slipped over her left nipple. He sucked her tender flesh between his lips and the pressure was so sweet and strong that an arrow of pleasure zinged right down to where Brady's mouth was now melting over her pussy.

Oh yes, this sure does beat working today.

JJ moaned as three tongues made love to her. She bucked and gasped as pleasure zipped and zapped throughout her body. The destructive combination and heat and pressure of their sensual mouths had her keening.

Their answering growls were like erotic music as the sounds filtered through the air.

Brady's tongue gently swirled around her pussy folds and then flicked like a snapping whip against her clit. She bucked and groaned beneath the erotic assault.

Dan's kiss intensified sparking more pleasure and when Rafe moved his mouth to her other nipple and began a harsh suckling, the tangled pleasure and sultry pain made her explode.

Heated blood and desire roared through her in tumultuous waves. Water splashed around her while she gyrated her hips against their forceful mouths. She shuddered and screamed and sucked in deep breaths as a penetrating orgasm raced through her with lightning speed.

She drowned within the sensations. Convulsed and tensed and shuddered.

Such gorgeous pleasure. Such wonderful cowboys.

Just thinking about them filled her heart with such a fierce love that she knew these guys were permanent.

They were hers. All hers.

Forever.

More Cowboys Online

~ Jan Springer ~ Erotic Romance ~

Cowboys for Christmas
Cowboys Online 1 ~ Moose Ranch

Jennifer Jane (JJ) Watson has spent the past ten Christmases in a maximum-security prison.

The last thing she expects is to get early parole, along with a job on a remote Canadian cattle ranch serving Christmas holiday dinners to three of the sexiest cowboys she's ever met!

Rafe, Brady and Dan thought they were getting a couple of male ex-cons to help out around their secluded ranch, but instead they get an attractive and very appealing female.

In the snowbound wilds of Northern Ontario, female companionship is rare.

It's a good thing the three men like to share...

They're dominating, sexy-as-sin and they fill JJ with the hottest ménage fantasies she's ever had. Suddenly she's craving cowboys for Christmas and wishing for something she knows she can never have...a happily ever after.

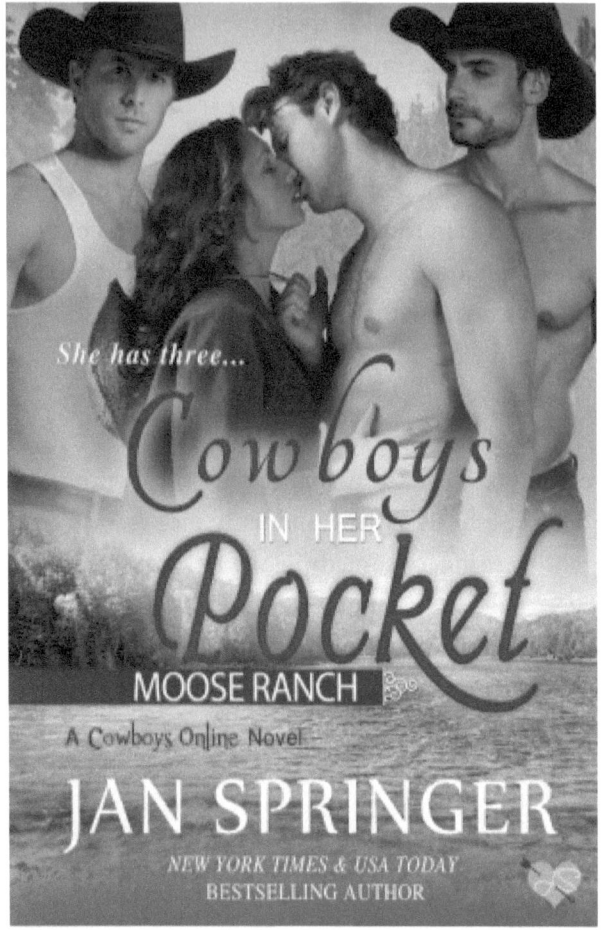

Cowboys In Her Pocket
Cowboys Online 2 ~ Moose Ranch
Jan Springer

*After spending ten years in a maximum-security prison Jennifer Jane (JJ)
Watson got early parole and a job on a remote Canadian cattle ranch
playing housekeeper to three of the sexiest cowboys she's ever met...*

Spring has finally arrived at Moose Ranch, and a single woman fresh
out of prison shouldn't be experiencing scorching ménages with her
three sexy-as-sin cowboys. But JJ's love for her men continues to grow

as she gives into the fevered heat and scorching passions she feels for each of them.

Life is perfect.

Until her new life is tested when mysterious happenings occur on the ranch and then one of her cowboys is viciously attacked and injured.

Will JJ's newfound freedom and happiness be ripped away?

Rafe, Brady and Dan never expected to find an attractive and very appealing female to help them out at their secluded ranch. But in the wilds of Northern Ontario, female companionship is rare. It's a good thing the three men like to share...

Brady, Dan and Rafe have never been happier. Their cattle ranch is flourishing and their continued desire to share the sexy woman who cares for them makes their life complete. Until danger threatens to rip everything apart...

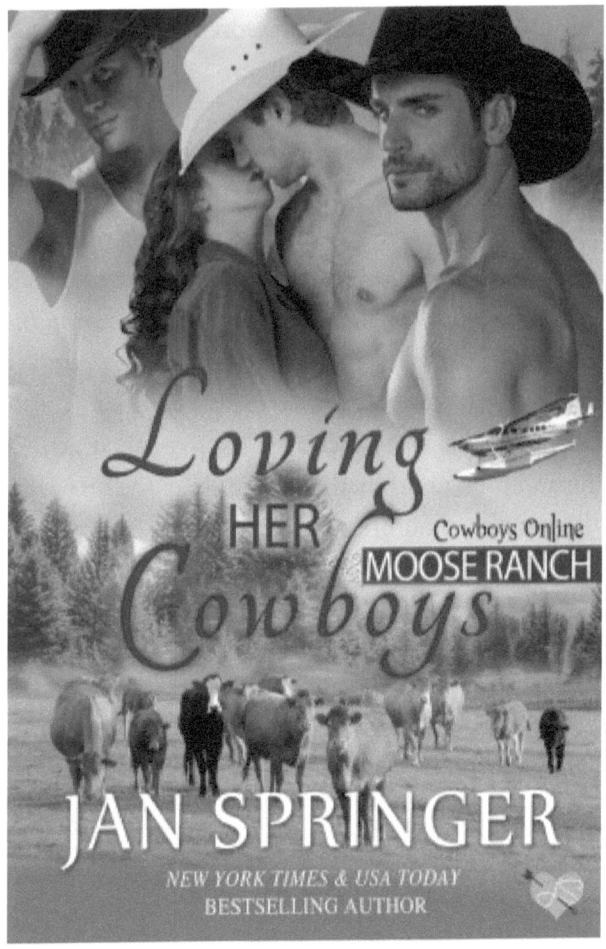

Loving Her Cowboys
Cowboys Online 3 ~ Moose Ranch
Jan Springer

AFTER SPENDING TEN years in a maximum-security prison Jennifer Jane (JJ) Watson got early parole and a job on a remote Canadian cattle ranch playing housekeeper to three of the sexiest cowboys she's ever met...

Her love for her cowboys continues to grow as she gives into fevered heat. But JJ's simmering restlessness explodes and she's seriously making up for lost time by pursuing her dreams. There's only one little problem. She hasn't revealed to her bosses what she's been up to while they're away tending to the cattle. She knows when they discover her secret, there will be hell to pay.

Ranchers Rafe, Dan and Brady have found the woman who completes them. She makes their secluded ranch a home-sweet-home. She's vulnerable, sweet and willing to share her bed with all three of them. But when JJ's secret is unwittingly revealed, they're stunned and angry. They figure it's time to dole out some fiery punishment in some mighty naughty ways...

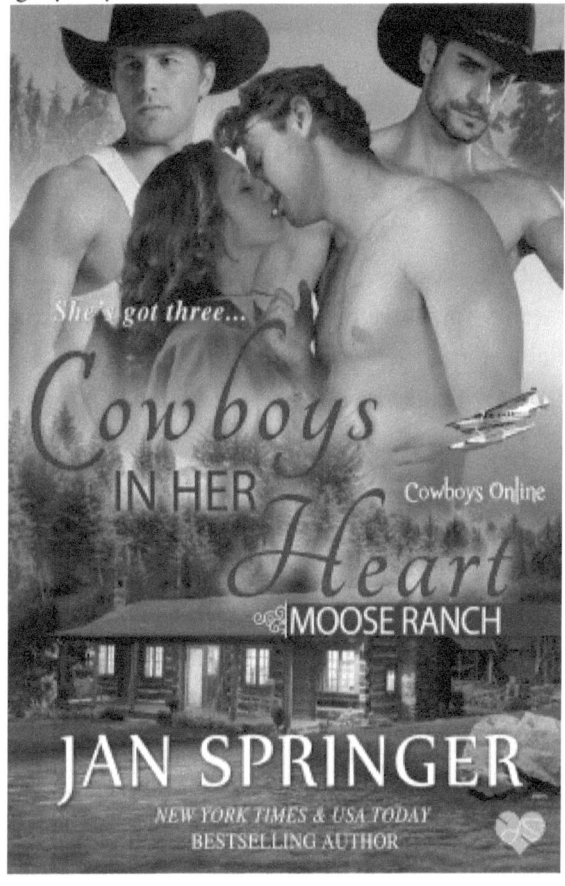

Cowboys In Her Heart
Cowboys Online 4 ~ Moose Ranch
Jan Springer

AFTER SPENDING TEN years in a maximum-security prison, JJ gets unexpected parole and a job on a Canadian ranch serving up scrumptious dinners and lots of hot love to three of the sexiest cowboys she's ever met.

Jennifer Jane "JJ" Watson has never been happier. She's going to have a baby!

Thankfully their wilderness ranch is a nice distraction for her three sexy cowboys while she's away flying her plane. But when she's home, her dominant hunks are tending to her naughty pregnant cravings and that includes plenty of sizzling ménages.

Rafe, Brady and Dan don't much like the idea of their woman flying the Canadian skies and being at the mercy of the unpredictable Northern Ontario weather. They would prefer having her warming their beds twenty-four seven. But she has a way of getting what she wants and right now she needs her new-found freedom.

Worst fears are realized when JJ, her friend and JJ's plane suddenly go missing and she doesn't come back home to them.

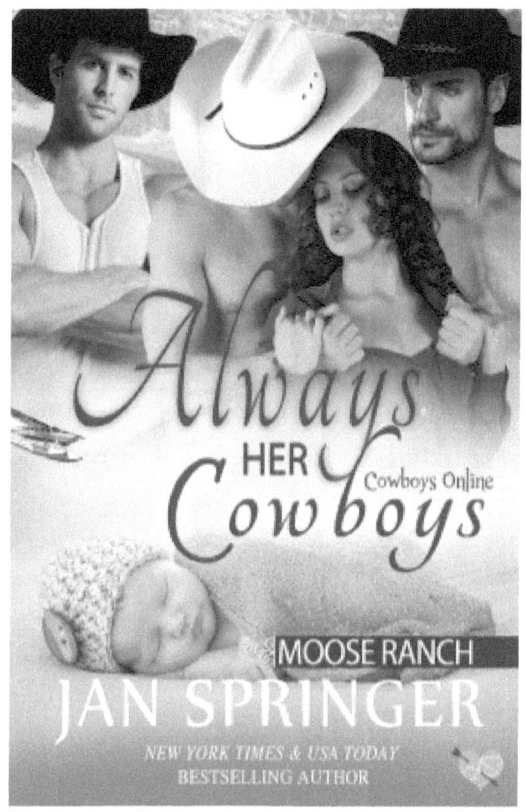

Always Her Cowboys
Cowboys Online #5 ~ Moose Ranch
A Canadian Contemporary Ménage Romance m/f/m/m

JENNIFER JANE (JJ) Watson has spent ten Christmases in a maximum-security prison. The last thing she expects is to get early parole, along with a job on a remote Canadian cattle ranch serving Christmas holiday dinners to three of the sexiest cowboys she's ever met!

Rafe, Brady and Dan thought they were getting male ex-cons to help out around their secluded ranch, but instead they get an attractive and very appealing female. In the snowbound wilds of Northern Ontario, female companionship is rare. It's a good thing the three men like to share...

Christmas is coming once again to Moose Ranch and with the due date of JJ's baby approaching fast, JJ is distracting herself from anxiety attacks by keeping herself ultra-busy preparing for the arrival of her baby and planning Moose Ranch's first annual Christmas party!

In having a wee baby on the way, there's a lot of stress for Brady, Rafe and Dan. Especially due to JJ's decision on having a wilderness mid-wife deliver the baby at the ranch house - *with* all *of them present for the birth*! But their concerns don't stop the men from showing JJ how much they love her...out of bed and in!

With wicked snowstorms, a grounded bush plane, a cheerful holiday party and a sweet little baby, the owners of Moose Ranch know this will be one sparkling Christmas season they won't soon forget...

Jan Springer Mini Catalog

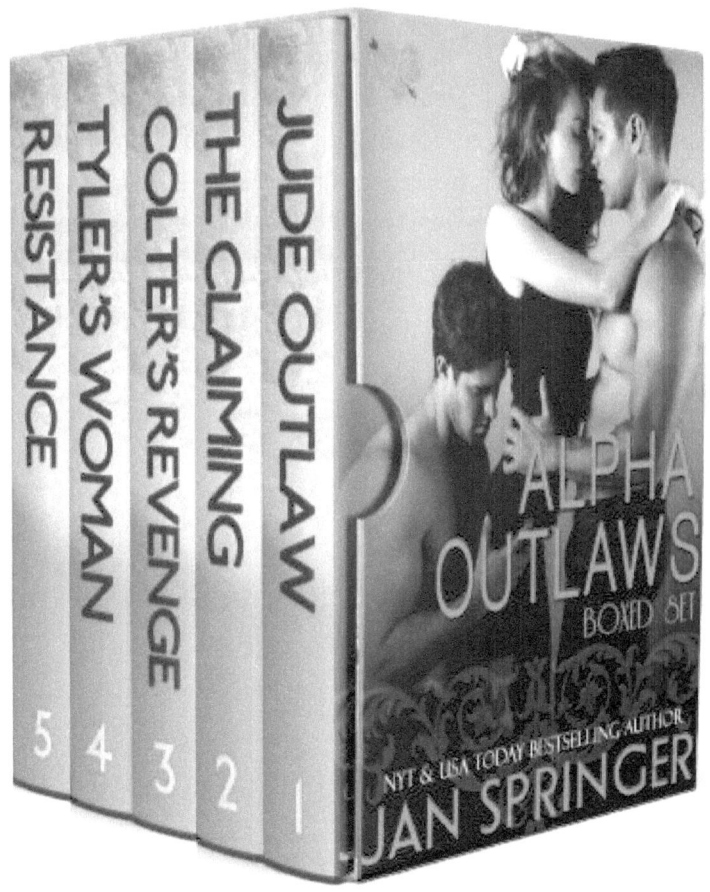

Alpha Outlaws Boxed Set
The Outlaw Lovers (Books 1 - 5)
A FAST-ACTING VIRUS has killed a majority of the world's female population. With so few women on Earth, a new law is created. The

Claiming Law allow groups of men to stake a claim on a female—as their sensual property.

The Outlaw brothers have full intentions of declaring ownership of the women they love...and they'll do it any way they can.

This boxed set contains the first FIVE books in The Outlaw Lovers series.

Jude Outlaw, The Claiming, Colter's Revenge, Tyler's Woman, Resistance,

Some scenes include scorching ménages, romances, light bondage, bdsm, m/f/m/m, m/f, m/f/m, m/m, anal, oral, double penetration, figging, and more...

Please note: Tyler's Woman Book 4 in this series is not for sensitive readers.

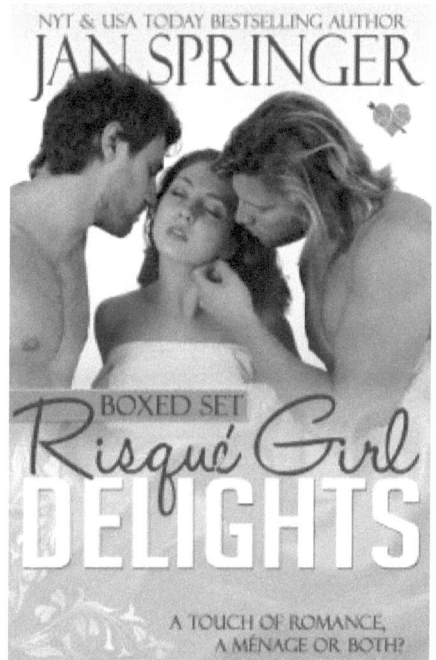

Risqué Girl Delights Box Set
A sizzling set of 4 contemporary erotic romances...Four women dare
to step out of the norm in the Risqué Girl Delights Boxed Set.
Includes sexy romances, naughty ménages, toys and hot alpha males.
Books: Edible Delights, Toygasm, Shy Girl, plus Roman & Julietta.
Edible Delights

YEARS AGO ALLIE MASTERS lost herself in the scorching passion
of a ménage a trois relationship with her two bosses. In order to regain
her independence, she walked away.

Max and Nick were very fulfilled with their gorgeous assistant.
The lovemaking was breathtaking and both men willingly shared the
woman they wanted to spend the rest of their lives with. Then she left.

Now Max and Nick have decided it's time to seduce Allie back into
their lives.

Toygasm

IT'S A CASE OF MISTAKEN identity when the two owners of Sexy Toys, show up for an erotic several day photo shoot of their toys with famous nude model Cammie Creek.

Cammie believes the two hunks are the male models she's supposed to work with. Usually she doesn't mix business with pleasure, but when they're seducing her right there in front of the camera, she can't resist turning them into her own personal naughty toys.

Josh and Jode are enjoying the perks of being male models; hot lust, sizzling toys and the best pleasure they've ever had. But how will Cammie react when she discovers they're actually her bosses and not just male models?

Shy Girl

FINALLY FREE OF AN abusive relationship, "Shy Girl" Emma McCall sheds her inhibitions and explores her sensual side at Club Rendezvous, a club specializing in the Alternate Lifestyle.

At the club she's surprised to find Logan Masters, a sexy hunk she's secretly fantasized about since college. With Logan's help, Emma will experience her ultimate fantasy - a scorching ménage a trois.

Roman and Julietta

HER PERFECT LOVER...

Modern day pirate Julietta Black's life has always been immersed in the violent and traditional ways of piracy. When her family's arch enemy puts a hit out on her family, Julietta knows there's only one way to lift the hit; she must kidnap the enemy's sexy grandson and force a union between the two warring families. Night after night, wrapped in Roman's strong arms, she can't deny the searing attraction blazing between them. Nor can she deny he now holds her heart as well as her life in his hands.

His dream angel...

When Roman Prince's mysterious captor offers him a luscious woman to bed, fierce desire ignites, melting his usually tight self-control. Lust quickly turns to love as he enjoys their naughty trysts more than he should. How will he react when he discovers he's been kidnapped, not for a ransom, but captured for his sperm?

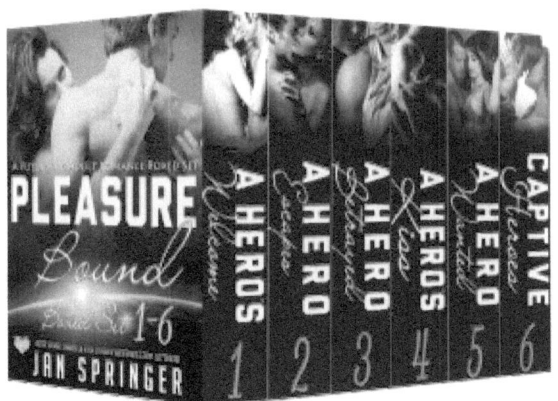

Futuristic Erotic Romance (m/f)
Pleasure Bound ~ The Complete Set ~ Books 1-6

A HERO'S WELCOME – Book One – Dr. Annie welcomes injured astronaut Joe Hero into her bed every chance she gets.

A Hero Escapes – Book Two – Queen Jacey's forbidden fantasies become reality and she can't get enough of well-hung Ben Hero's sizzling lovemaking.

A Hero Betrayed – Book Three – Fugitive-on-the-run Virgin must save Buck Hero who has been infected by a deadly virus. The cure? A twenty-four-hour making love marathon! But then she must betray him...

A Hero's Kiss – Book Four – US Astronaut Piper Hero is rescued by a dangerous stranger and can't seem to keep her hands off his luscious whip-scarred body.

A Hero Wanted – Book Five – A Hero is wanted for plus-sized Jenna who is finally able to explore her intimate side...where ménages are welcome.

Captive Heroes – Book Six – While searching for her brothers, Kayla Hero is bound and imprisoned by the Breeders— along with a male captive whose tantalizing scars pique her interest.

Injured and lost in a dense jungle, Kinley Hero is intimidated by the scarred man who hunts her, especially due to the power of erotic submission he holds over her.

Naughty Girl Desires Boxed Set
Contemporary Erotic Romance (m/f)
Includes: Jade's Fantasy, The Biker & The Bride,
Sinderella Sexy and Nice Girl Naughty.

Jade's Fantasy
*In the land of the rich and famous, Kidnap Fantasies is the answer to
discreet naughty downtime.*
When ex-downhill skier Jade Hart's two sisters give her a Kidnap
Fantasies questionnaire, Jade is aroused at the prospect of having
no-strings fun in the sun with a stranger whose only job would be to
fulfill her every intimate fantasy. Although she knows she's too shy to
send it in, she secretly pours her deepest wishes into the questionnaire.
Soon the questionnaire mysteriously vanishes and Jade's fantasy man
appears on her luxury yacht in the form of a sexy handy man who gives
her an intimate toy-filled Christmas holiday she'll never forget.

The Biker & The Bride
Wrapped in red-hot lust for revenge, Avery plots to murder the man
responsible for the death of her son.
Her plans are dashed when her ex-husband crashes her wedding and
whisks her away on his motorcycle to the rustic Canadian wilderness
cabin they'd once honeymooned.
Police detective, Mason is fighting for Avery's love with everything he
has.
Armed with whipped cream, handcuffs and his undying devotion,
Mason vows he will make Avery love again.

But it's only a matter of time before the man she'd planned to kill hunts them down...

Sinderella Sexy

By night, Dr. Ella Cinder, escapes reality by secretly performing in her own naughty version of Cinderella, aptly re-titled Sinderella. When sexy colleague Dr. Roarke Stephenson appears in the Sinderella audience on the same night her Prince Charming stands her up, Ella Cinder seizes the opportunity to make the man she's secretly fantasized about into her very own Prince Charming for one night of carnal fun in front of an audience.

But at the stroke of midnight, Ella knows she must face the harsh reality that Roarke can never learn her true identity.

Dr. Roarke Stephenson is immediately captured by the mysterious actress who hides her face behind a mask and is known only as Sinderella. For some insane reason, she reminds him of his klutzy co-worker, Ella. But that's not possible. Plain Ella would never have the nerve to do the wickedly delicious things Sinderella does to him, or would she?

Nice Girl Naughty

Blind since nineteen, Summer has blossomed into a famous wood carver.

When she's almost killed by a serial killer, she's whisked away to a secluded wilderness cabin by the man she once secretly loved. Summer can't get enough of touching professional bodyguard Nick Cassidy's thick, powerful muscles and all those other hard, yummy male body parts that she has always longed to explore.

For years Nick has stayed away from his best friend's kid sister, nice girl Summer. Now he's back, and sweeping his gorgeous redhead into the naughty cravings he's always had for her. With passion blinding him, Nick doesn't realize their hideout isn't safe—until it's too late.

YOU CAN GET A PEEK at more of Jan Springer's Erotic Romances at:

http://www.janspringer.com[1]

---

1.   http://www.janspringer.com/

Jan's Newsletter

Hi! If you would like to get an email when my books are released, you can sign up here:

English Newsletter: http://ymlp.com/xguembmugmgb

Italian Newsletter: https://ymlp.com/xgwsuysygmgj

Your email addresses will never be shared and you can unsubscribe whenever you like.

Jasmine Black

Taken By Two Billionaires
Jasmine Black

Jill has always been warned that her gambling lifestyle would get her into trouble. And now *she's in trouble*.

She's lost a poker game to two very sexy billionaires and they want *her* as their winnings.

They'll to do her whatever they wish...for an entire year.

On her way to her new life in Italy, while in a white stretch limo, Franco and Gianni will show Jill exactly what it means *to be won* by two billionaires.

Other eBooks in the Taken series
Taken by Two Physical Trainers
Taken by Two Firefighters
Taken by Two Bikers
Taken by Two Bosses
Taken by Two Cowboys
Taken by Two Doctors
Taken by Three Doctors
Taken by Three Bikers
Taken by Three Billionaires

Jasmine Black Website ~ http://www.jasmine-black.com
Twitter ~ @blackerotica1
Jasmine Black Newsletter ~ http://ymlp.com/xghwwwmugmgj

ABOUT THE AUTHOR

Jan Springer writes full-time at her home nestled in cottage country, Ontario, Canada. She enjoys hiking, kayaking, gardening, reading and writing. She is a member of the Romance Writers of America.

Here are other ways you can connect with Jan Springer:

Jan Springer Website at http://www.janspringer.com[1]

Instagram – http://www.instagram.com/janspringerauthor

Facebook - https://www.facebook.com/janspringereroticromance

Twitter - https://twitter.com/janspringer @janspringer

Pinterest - http://www.pinterest.com/janspringer1/

Jan's Blog - http://janspringerauthor.wordpress.com/blog-2/

LinkedIn - http://ca.linkedin.com/in/janspringerauthor/

Google   Plus   -   https://plus.google.com/u/0/101527334949931513035/posts

Goodreads   -   https://www.goodreads.com/author/show/260628.Jan_Springer

Happy Reading,
Jan Springer

Don't miss out!

Visit the website below and you can sign up to receive emails whenever Jan Springer publishes a new book. There's no charge and no obligation.

https://books2read.com/r/B-A-WGQ-MLWO

BOOKS 2 READ

Connecting independent readers to independent writers.

www.ingramcontent.com/pod-product-compliance
Lightning Source LLC
Chambersburg PA
CBHW020812060726
47498CB00017B/2770